THE MOON'S ON FIRE

Margaret Donaldson

Illustrated by Joanna Stubbs

Hippo Books
Scholastic Publications Limited
London

Scholastic Publications Ltd,
141-143 Drury Lane, London WC2B 5TG England

Scholastic Book Services,
50 West 44th Street, New York 10036 NY USA

Scholastic Tab Publications Ltd,
123 Newkirk Road, Richmond Hill, Ontario L4C 3G5
Canada

H J Ashton Co Pty Ltd, Box 579,
Gosford, New South Wales, Australia

H J Ashton Co Pty Ltd,
9-11 Fairfax Avenue, Penrose, Auckland, New Zealand

First published by André Deutsch Ltd 1980
Published by Scholastic Publications Ltd 1981
Copyright © 1980 by Margaret Donaldson
Illustrations copyright © 1980 by Joanna Stubbs
All rights reserved

Typeset by Computacomp (UK) Ltd, Fort William, Scotland
Made and printed in the USA
Set in Baskerville

Chapter 1

"It's on fire! It's going to crash!" said Tadek in a loud whisper and rose up from his seat. The German bomber turned its nose downward and began to fall helplessly into an English cornfield. Smoke from its wings streaked the sky.

"Sit down, Tadek!" said Mr Sharcus. "The people behind you won't be able to see."

And Janey's Aunt Sarah whispered from the other side of him: "Do be quiet! I know it's exciting but you mustn't make a noise in the cinema."

Tadek sat down again. At home in Poland, he thought, people would cheer if they saw an enemy bomber going down in flames. Here in England you were always supposed to be quiet and sit still and not get excited. He did not like it.

The cinema screen showed more planes in the sky – Spitfires this time – and then a shot of the cliffs of Dover and the English Channel.

"Hitler's troops are waiting across the Channel in France, ready for the order to invade us," said the voice of the commentator. "But Hitler wants to be sure that they will have an easy time when they come. And it's not only our men in the air force and the navy who can stop that from happening. We can all help, every one of us."

"How?" Tadek wondered. And his twin brother, Stefek, farther along the row, was wondering exactly the same thing.

There was a picture now of German tanks

5

rolling along a straight road lined with poplar trees. Janey, who was sitting beside her aunt, watched it and shivered. "That picture was taken in France," she thought, remembering what it had been like there when the Germans came.

The tanks vanished and Hitler himself appeared on the screen, making a speech to a great

crowd of people. His voice grew louder and louder until he was screaming, and the crowd roared back at him. "Sieg Heil!" they roared and stuck out their arms in the Nazi salute.

"That is what we have to stop," the commentator was saying. "And we all know what happened in Holland and in France. When the German soldiers came, Hitler's friends inside those countries were waiting to give help. We must make sure it doesn't happen here. We must look out for spies and traitors in our midst."

Now the screen showed a picture of a dark

street with a light flashing at a window.

"If you ever see something like this," said the voice, "remember that it could be a signal and that you should tell the police about it. Every one of us is a fighter against the enemies who are among us, Hitler's Fifth Column. If we all watch out for anything suspicious, we shall be helping our soldiers and sailors and airmen to win the war."

The film ended, the lights went up and the cinema organ began to play.

"What's that tune, Aunt Sarah?" Janey asked.

"It's called 'Deep Purple'," her aunt told her. "Haven't you heard it before? It's not new. But then you've only been back from France for a month or two. I keep forgetting there are lots of things you may not know."

"It's a funny name for a tune," said Janey. "How would you say that in Polish, Tadek?"

But Tadek wasn't listening. He was thinking about spies. And his twin brother, Stefek, farther along the row, was doing exactly the same thing.

"Should we go and tell the police?" Tadek asked that night when they were in bed. But Stefek did not think so.

"The police probably wouldn't believe us," he said. "I think we need more evidence first."

"Well, how are we going to get it?" Tadek wondered.

A noise came from downstairs, a single thud like the big front door closing.

"Listen!" said Stefek. "That's him going out again. What time is it?"

Tadek reached over and switched on his bed lamp.

"Three minutes past ten. So why does he go out

every night at the same time?"

"He says he likes to take a walk."

"Even when the streets are blacked out and there could be an air raid any minute?"

"Well, you know what he says," Stefek answered. "He says he isn't going to let this war change his whole life. He says he has always taken a quiet walk alone before going to bed and he means to continue to do so."

Stefek imitated the way Mr Sharcus spoke. Tadek laughed.

"That would be a good excuse, wouldn't it, though?" he said. "It would be very easy for him to meet another spy in the darkness and pass messages. We really have to do something, you know. Remember what the man said in that film. It's our duty."

Stefek agreed. "All right, I tell you what. Tomorrow night one of us will follow him. We'll climb out through Janey's window and hide in the garden until he comes. Then we'll follow him and see where he goes."

"Who'll be first?" said Tadek eagerly.

"We'll toss a penny," said Stefek. "Wait a minute."

He found a penny in his pocket and tossed it. Tadek won.

"He's a funny man, isn't he?" Tadek murmured as they were falling asleep a little later. "His two eyes aren't the same colour. One's a darker blue than the other. Did you notice?"

"What's that got to do with it?" said Stefek in a voice that was muffled by the blankets over his head.

"I don't know," said Tadek. "Just that there's something funny about him, that's all."

Chapter 2

"But you don't *really* think he's a spy, do you?" said Janey. She stopped walking and wrinkled her forehead. The idea that her uncle might be spying for the Germans upset her – even if he wasn't her real uncle but only someone Aunt Sarah had married a year ago.

"Why not?" said Tadek. "He's a funny sort of man, isn't he? And he doesn't approve of the war, you know. He thinks England should stop fighting Hitler, I've heard him say so."

Janey sat down on the grass under an elm tree and tried to imagine Uncle Maurice as a spy. Stefek came to stand beside her, his hands stuffed deep into his trouser pockets. Tadek lay down on the ground near them with his heels kicking in the air.

"Uncle Maurice doesn't think people should go fighting and killing each other," said Janey slowly. "And then he's worried about his business, you know. The wine that he sells comes from France and Germany mainly. He can't get any at all now, except when a ship comes in from Portugal and that's not often. He thinks he won't have any money left if the war goes on."

Tadek twisted round and sat up suddenly with a fierce scowl on his face.

"That's all your uncle Mr stupid old Maurice Sharcus, the wicked Shark, cares about!" he cried. "His silly wine and his money. The Shark doesn't care about the countries that have been attacked and the people that have been killed and

9

taken away by the Germans. I don't believe he cares about them at all or he wouldn't say we should stop fighting Hitler! Of course it's not good for people to go fighting and killing each other but who started it?"

Tadek's face, which had been red at first, was now pale. He let himself slide back to the ground again and he lay there stiffly, watching the sky. Three fighter planes came from behind a cloud, heading in the direction of the Kent coast.

"Hurricanes," said Stefek.

Up in the tree, a blackbird was singing.

"I'm sorry, Tadek," said Janey quietly. "I didn't mean ..." For she knew that Tadek was thinking about his father, who had been killed when the German army invaded Poland, and about his mother, who had been taken away from home in the middle of the night and who had not come back again.

"It's all right, Janey," Tadek told her. "I'm not angry with you." But he did not look round, he just went on staring at the sky.

"The Shark *is* a funny man, you know," Stefek said. "He's even got a funny name. 'Sharcus' doesn't sound very English, does it? Where does he come from?"

"I don't know," Janey admitted. "I never thought about it. I've never asked anyone. But he speaks like an Englishman, doesn't he?"

"That doesn't mean a thing," said Stefek. "We speak like English boys because our mother was English, and yet our father was Polish and we were born in Poland. You can speak French like a French girl because you lived there for years but both your parents were English. So it doesn't mean a thing, you know."

They left the park and went home for tea. Aunt Sarah was in the kitchen boiling the kettle. Janey went to speak to her while the boys were still outside in the garden.

"Where does Uncle Maurice come from?" said Janey, trying to make the question sound quite ordinary.

"From Bristol," said Aunt Sarah. "Put some water in the teapot to warm it, will you please, Janey? Be careful not to scald yourself. Can you manage?"

Janey thought: "Of course I can manage. How does she suppose I managed when I was all alone in France with the German soldiers coming?"

Out loud she said: "I never heard the name 'Sharcus' until you married Uncle Maurice. It's not an English name, is it?"

11

As Janey spoke, Aunt Sarah was pouring milk into a jug. She looked up quickly with a slight frown on her face and a few drops of milk ran over the side.

"What makes you ask that, Jane?" she said.

Janey felt herself blushing.

"I just wondered," she answered uneasily. "It *is* a funny name."

Aunt Sarah wiped up the milk, put the jug on the tray and rubbed her back as if it hurt her.

"I don't know where the name came from originally," she said, "but your uncle's family has been in England for a long time. Now go and call the boys and we'll have tea."

After tea the twins went out to the garden and began to play croquet, or at least to practise knocking balls through a hoop, but Janey would not join them. She went up to her room and sat on the window seat trying to think things out. *Could* Uncle Maurice be a spy?

What she wished most was that she could talk to her father about it. But her father had gone back to France to work with his friends there who were fighting the Germans, and she had no way of getting in touch with him.

She began to think about the day he went away – the day when he left her and the twins with Uncle Maurice and Aunt Sarah. She remembered how they had all had lunch together and how Uncle Maurice had spoken about his wine, as he usually did, grumbling because he would soon have none left to sell. And Janey's father had told him:

"Maurice, you don't know how lucky you are, sitting here in this comfortable house of yours. Can you imagine what it would be like to have to leave it, as I had to leave my house in France, because the German tanks were a couple of miles from the door?"

Janey was sure of one thing: her father had not suspected that Uncle Maurice was a spy. But perhaps he had not known about the walks every evening after dark which worried the twins so much.

She began to think about Uncle Maurice's name. "Maurice" could be English or it could be French — not German as far as she knew.

Then she remembered that he had a middle name, but she did not know what is was, only that it began with the letter "H". "Maurice H. Sharcus Ltd." — that was the name of his firm. If she could find out what "H" stood for, that might help.

She wondered which German names began with "H" and at once she thought of "Hermann". As soon as this came into her mind, she found herself full of a terrible fear that her uncle was called "Maurice Hermann Sharcus". She began to say it over to herself and it sounded right. The more she said it, the more convincing it seemed. She tried desperately to put "Henry" in the middle instead, but "Hermann" wouldn't go away.

There was only one thing to do, then: she had to find out. And there was only one way to find out that she could think of, since she did not dare to ask Aunt Sarah any more questions. She would have to look at her uncle's passport.

A few days before, Janey had been in his study and she had seen the passport lying on his desk. She decided to go to the study at once, before he got home.

The boys were still in the garden, which was

good. She did not want them with her. She could hear their voices and the clunk of the croquet mallet as it hit the ball. Aunt Sarah would be in her own little sitting-room, reading a book or knitting something for the sailors or the airmen – or perhaps for the baby that she was going to have soon. It was a good time. There would never be a better one.

Janey uncurled her legs and ran across the room. Outside, she stood listening, but everything in the house was quiet. She went downstairs, tiptoed through the hall and opened the study door.

Uncle Maurice turned in his chair at the desk to look at her.

"Jane!" he said. "What are you doing here?"

For a moment Janey was too surprised to speak. Then she managed to stammer: .

"I'm s – sorry. I didn't know you had come home."

"I can see that," said Uncle Maurice, and there was a puzzled look on his face. "What do you want, Jane?"

"I – I came to look up a word in your dictionary," Janey told him. She felt her face flushing red.

"What is the word?" said Uncle Maurice.

Janey searched for a word frantically.

"Sp–" she began. "Er – no – I mean – er – shark."

"Shark?" said Uncle Maurice, looking more puzzled than ever. "But you know what 'shark' means, don't you?"

"Yes, but I want to find out more about them," said Janey miserably.

"Then you need an encyclopaedia, not a dictionary."

He got up, crossed to one of the bookshelves and took down a big book in dark red leather binding. "Volume 24, SAI TO SHU." He opened it and turned some pages. "Here we are. Page 805. *Shark*, a Selachian fish (see SELACHIANS) belonging to the order Plagiostomi, suborder Squali. Does that help?"

He raised his eyebrows and looked at her without smiling.

"There are four pages about sharks here," he said, "and lots of pictures of them. You may borrow the book, Jane, but take good care of it. It's the *Encyclopaedia Britannica*, the eleventh edition, and it's valuable, you understand. And will you ask me or your Aunt Sarah if you want to borrow a book from here again?"

Janey gulped, thanked him and promised. As she turned to leave the room, a rumbling noise reached their ears, like thunder from far away.

whole of London!

Was it a signal? Did the Shark know that the bombers were coming? Could he be trying to guide them? Was that why he hadn't come out as usual?

Tadek did not know what to do. He was supposed to stay at his post and do his job. If he ran off now and looked for an air raid warden, the Shark might come out after all and get away. But that light! He couldn't just stand and watch that light! Something had to be done, and quickly.

He ran out from behind the bushes and turned towards the gate. He would go to the house across the road, ring the door bell there, tell them to—

He stopped suddenly as he remembered the soot on his face. Well, then, he would ring the bell and run away. As soon as they came to the door they would see the light and they would fetch the air raid warden themselves. There would be no need to tell them anything.

He was halfway across the road when he heard the shout:

"Hey! That light! Get that light out!"

He dodged away into the shelter of the opposite wall and crouched there as the warden's heavy feet came pounding along the pavement and the warden's fist thundered on the Shark's door.

"You in there! Don't you know there's a war on? Get that flaming light out! Do you want a bomb on your head?"

The light clicked out. A moment later the front door opened and Tadek heard a voice speaking. It was the Shark all right, but it was impossible to hear what he was saying. The words of the angry warden, however, were still very clear:

"You know you could go to prison for this? You will too, if it happens again. I swear you will, if I have anything to do with it!"

Tadek could not help wishing that it would happen again − so long as it didn't help the Germans.

He heard the door closing. The warden was leaving now, stumping angrily down the path and off along the road.

Tadek stayed where he was until everything was quiet again. Then he went back to his hiding-place in the bushes. He would wait for another half-hour, he decided. The Shark might still come.

Chapter 4

Janey's room was at the back of the house, above an outbuilding that was only a single storey high. It was easy to reach the roof of this outhouse by climbing up a drainpipe and then it was easy to reach Janey's window-sill. Tadek crouched there and rapped on the glass gently. After a second or two the window was opened for him and he climbed in.

"What happened?" Janey whispered before he was fully inside. But he did not tell her at once. Instead he turned to close the window behind him and make sure that the heavy curtain was back in its place. Even then, he asked a question instead of answering hers.

"Did you hear that row about the light?" he said.

His brother Stefek switched on the lamp.

"Tadek," he said, "you know quite well we heard the row. We couldn't help hearing it. Why don't you tell us what happened?"

Tadek sighed.

"Because nothing happened, that's why!" he muttered. He pulled off the woollen cap and smoothed down his fair hair, making sooty streaks on it.

"You mean the Shark didn't come out?" said Janey.

"Oh, he came out in the end. But then nothing happened. He went for a walk, that's all. He went round the – round the houses."

"You mean round the block," said Janey, without stopping to think. Then she wished she had said nothing, for Tadek scowled. And when he spoke he sounded even more unhappy than before.

"That's it. Round the block," he said. "Twice. Nothing more."

Janey knew very well why Tadek was upset. He was proud of the way he could speak English and he spoke it very well. But the twins had come to live in England only three months before, and sometimes they found that they did not know exactly the right word. Tadek especially was annoyed when this happened to him. And now of course he was in a bad mood anyway because he had found no evidence that the Shark was a spy.

21

Janey was thankful for this. She tried "Maurice Hermann Sharcus" in her mind again and it sounded much less likely now, which was a great relief to her. But Stefek was not ready to believe that the Shark was innocent.

"He didn't meet anyone?" he persisted.

"No one at all."

"You're sure you would have seen if he had?"

"Quite sure."

"Could he have left a message anywhere, in a secret place for someone to pick up?"

Tadek thought for a moment before he answered. He was sitting now cross-legged on the floor.

"That's possible," he admitted. "That's just possible if he did it quickly."

"He could have dropped a note into a litter bin, for instance," said Stefek, growing pleased with his idea. "Someone might have been waiting to pick it up after he'd gone by. In that case they probably saw you coming after him."

This suggestion made Tadek feel worse than ever. His scowl grew deeper. He stared at his feet.

"You know," said Janey slowly, "I don't believe he's a spy at all. If he *was* a spy, do you think he'd say all those things about the war? He'd be more likely to pretend to *hate* the Germans, wouldn't he?"

"I've no idea!" Tadek snapped angrily. "I don't know what he'd do. I only know he's a rotten Nazi! And what I can't understand is why your aunt married him." He rose suddenly to his feet. "I'm tired now. Come on, Stefek. I want to go to bed."

"Tomorrow," said Stefek, "it will be my turn to follow him."

After the twins had gone, Janey lay awake thinking. "Why *did* Aunt Sarah marry him?" she wondered. But she couldn't understand it either. Perhaps the Shark wasn't exactly a spy but she could not make herself like him much. He was quite kind sometimes, she had to admit that. He had been quite kind when she went into the study. Some people might have got very angry. But she had a feeling that he had almost got very angry and had only just managed to control it.

"Perhaps he doesn't like children," she thought.

She knew he certainly did not like having the twins to live with him. One day, as she passed an open door, she had heard something which worried her. Uncle Maurice was speaking to Aunt Sarah:

"I'm beginning to think we should never have taken those boys to live with us, Sarah, and perhaps your brother should never have asked us to have them. I'm afraid it's getting to be too much for you."

"It was difficult to know what to do, wasn't it?" Aunt Sarah replied. "They've had such a hard time, with their father killed and their mother missing and all those months wandering around Europe on their own. Besides, where else could they have gone?"

"There are work camps for refugees from Europe, aren't there?" Uncle Maurice reminded her. "You know, work camps where they could learn to do useful jobs."

"I suppose so," said Aunt Sarah doubtfully, "but the camps seem to be rather dreadful places. I was reading something about them in *The Times* the other day. I don't think we could really send the twins there. And it would make Janey so unhappy."

23

Yes, it would, Janey thought. She could not help listening to some more.

"Well, I really don't know," said Uncle Maurice. "I certainly don't want to insist on anything that would upset you, especially just now with the baby coming. But you'll have quite enough to do when he's born, you know, without looking after all those children too. And there's no hope of getting servants now because of this crazy war – even if we have any money to pay them, which we won't now that my business is ruined."

Janey had not told the twins about hearing this conversation, but it had worried her a great deal.

Chapter 5

Mr Sharcus finished the wine in his glass and raised his table napkin to his lips.

"I have only two more cases of this wine left," he said. "Would you believe it? Only two more cases of Gruaud-Larose in the whole of the Sharcus cellars! And when I think what will happen to this year's grapes I could weep! All over France they will rot on the vines unharvested because of this war. It's a tragedy!"

Stefek could not stay silent.

"What about the *people*?" he cried. "Don't you care about what is happening to them? Is it only grapes you care about?"

Mr Sharcus looked at him with sudden anger in his eyes.

"Don't be impertinent!" he said. "Of course I care about what is happening to the people. I hate this senseless killing. So I want the war to end. You've heard me say so."

"Yes, we have!" cried Tadek. "But you want to make it end by giving in to Hitler, and he's a wicked man. You want to let him get away with all he's done. You want to let him keep Poland and all the other countries that he has invaded. He *stole* those countries! It's wrong!"

Mr Sharcus pressed his lips together, folded his napkin and put it carefully into a silver ring.

"My dear," he said to his wife, "I'll take my coffee in the study this evening, please." Then, turning to Tadek:

"I suppose you're too young to understand, Tadek, and you've been badly hurt so I'll try to make allowances for your impertinence when you're a guest in my house."

He picked up the napkin again and began to twirl the ring round and round between his fingers.

"Things were very bad in Germany before Hitler came to power, you know. I don't say what he did was right but I do say it was understandable, and I believe he really doesn't want to attack us now. He said it very clearly in his speech to the Reichstag last month. 'It was never my intention to destroy or even to harm the British Empire.' These were his exact words, as reported in *The Times*."

Mr Sharcus pushed back his chair and rose to his feet, but he went on with the little speech he was making.

"I know that it's hard for you boys and for your country but, you see, war is like that." He began to walk up and down the dining-room floor. "War has always been like that. One country wins, another loses."

He swung round and looked at the twins with his blue eyes, one darker than the other.

"War is bad," he said. "War is always bad. And the sooner it's over the better."

When Janey's aunt carried the coffee into the study, her husband was sitting at his desk with a large book open in front of him and he was groaning.

"The stock is *so* low," he said. "There's next to nothing left! Next to nothing!"

Aunt Sarah did not believe it was as bad as that. Not long ago she had been in the big warehouse down by the docks and it was not empty. But she tried to think of something to cheer him up.

"Perhaps that ship will come from Portugal next week," she said. "What's the name of it?"

"The *San Domingo*," he told her. "But it won't get through. How can it? There are mines in the sea and bombers in the air and the Germans are shelling us from the other side of the Channel. How can it reach us?"

"Perhaps it will, all the same," she murmured soothingly. "Don't worry, Maurice, the war may soon be over."

"It's not likely, is it?" he said bitterly. "Not with that madman, Churchill, running the country. And we've really got no proper defence, you know. The Home Guard is a joke. If Hitler's invasion troops sailed tomorrow there would be nothing we could do. What puzzles me is why they haven't sailed already."

He took a sip of his coffee and looked at his wife.

"You know, Sarah," he said, "those boys really are beginning to annoy me. I try to keep my temper and make allowances for them, but there are times when it's almost more than I can do. And, do you know, I believe they're getting worse. Is it my imagination or is something going on in this house? Are those children up to something? Jane came into my study yesterday afternoon with a very funny story."

"What story?" Aunt Sarah asked.

"She said she wanted to look up the word 'shark' in a dictionary."

"The word 'shark'? How very odd!"

"That's what *I* thought. However, I gave her a volume of the *Encyclopaedia Britannica* to satisfy her. But it seemed to me that she looked very

27

embarrassed. I don't think she was telling the truth."

Aunt Sarah remembered Janey's flushed face in the kitchen when she was asking about the name "Sharcus". But she said nothing.

Stefek went out through the window and down the drainpipe at ten minutes past ten. An hour later Janey and Tadek were waiting restlessly for him to come back and Janey was wondering what would happen if anything went wrong. Janey had still not spoken to the twins about the work camps for refugees.

"Tomorrow," said Tadek, "I think that Stefek and I—" A loud noise from below made him stop suddenly. "What was that?"

"The front door?" Janey whispered.

Then they heard the Shark's voice. Usually it was not a loud voice and it did not carry far. Now he was shouting as they had never heard him shout before.

They ran quickly on to the landing, forgetting to take care. Downstairs in the hall, Stefek and the Shark stood facing one another while Aunt Sarah watched from the sitting-room door.

Aunt Sarah had been knitting a long scarf in navy blue wool and the knitting needles were still in her hands. She had let the ball drop to the floor and the end of the scarf was trailing round her ankles.

"She'll trip over it," Janey thought.

The Shark was trembling and spluttering with rage.

"What kind of nonsense is this?" he yelled. "Explain yourself, boy! What's the meaning of that filthy soot all over you? You were following me, weren't you? Creeping after me like that!

28

What's going on, eh? What's going on?"

Stefek was silent.

"I've taken you into my home and looked after you and this is how you thank me, is it?" the Shark cried. "Go into the study there at once! You're going to get the whipping you deserve!"

Stefek stood still, his eyes shining defiantly in his black face.

"I won't go," he said. "I won't take punishment from you. I've heard the things you say about the Germans and about Hitler. You *like* them! You're a Nazi! You're a spy!"

"I'm what? Come here! You little devil!" And the Shark took hold of him by the collar and pulled. But he was not a very big man and Stefek was strong.

"You little devil!" cried the Shark again, gasping and tugging, and growing still more furious. "I'll show you!"

He managed to drag Stefek several yards across the floor but he did not notice that the rug was being pulled up by Stefek's feet. A small table tumbled over and a glass ornament fell and broke in many pieces.

"Oh!" cried Aunt Sarah. "My lovely Thomas Webb vase! Oh!" She lifted her hands till the

scarf almost hid her face, as if she could not bear to look at what was happening.

"*Now* see what you've done, you wretched boy!" the Shark roared. "You scum! You filthy Polish scum! No wonder Hitler felt he had to clean up Europe!"

This was too much for Tadek. He gave a yell like a war-cry and raced down the stairs to join in.

"You're a Nazi!" he shouted. "A Nazi pig! Schweinhund!"

"Oh!" cried Aunt Sarah, "Oh, Maurice, take care! Don't hurt them!"

Janey ran downstairs too, behind Tadek. The Shark, who was still holding on to Stefek's collar, grabbed a walking-stick with his left hand and swung it threateningly. The end of the stick hit a wall mirror and shattered it. As the Shark turned to see what had happened, Stefek managed to twist himself free.

It was as if the Shark went mad then. He began to hit out wildly at the boys, who dodged him, round and round, in the hall. Another table crashed over.

"He'll murder them!" Janey thought desperately, as she watched the stick just miss Stefek's skull. Her aunt was trying to shout something to her but she could not make out what it was.

Then, without warning, the fight was over. Tadek came at the Shark from behind, grabbing his ankles. The man staggered and fell forward. Before he could get up, Stefek had the front door open.

"Out!" he yelled. "Out, Tadek, quick!"

Forgetting all about the black-out and the German bombers, the two of them raced away into the darkness.

Chapter 6

Janey's uncle telephoned for the police and a sergeant came round to see what had happened. Mr Sharcus told him that the boys were violent and out of control.

"Look at this, sergeant," he said, pointing to the mess in the hall, which he had refused to let Aunt Sarah tidy up. "And they must be found for their own sakes if nothing else, don't you see?"

"I see, sir. Yes, I do see," said the sergeant and he wrote something in his notebook.

The sergeant's two front teeth had a wide space between them. He put the end of his pencil neatly into the gap and sucked it for a moment. Then, taking it out again, he asked:

"Can you describe the young gentlemen, sir?"

"I'm afraid they're scarcely young gentlemen, more like hooligans," said Mr Sharcus. He was still very angry though he managed to seem quiet and calm again. "And they're foreigners, by the way," he added. "Not English, though they speak English well."

"Ah!" said the sergeant as if that explained everything. "For-eign-ers," he murmured, and he began to write again in the notebook. But he wrote slowly and hesitantly and Janey noticed that his ears grew pink. She thought: "He doesn't know how to spell it!"

"Now will you describe them, sir, if you please," the sergeant said.

"They're tall for their age – about five feet tall

31

in France which might spread to other animals. They called it "putting him in quarantine" and Janey understood that it was necessary, but she missed him badly and she knew she would miss him even more if the twins were not with her.

"What will you do?" she asked Stefek, without looking at him.

"I don't know," he replied. "We're worried about going away from here without finding out if the Shark is really a spy."

"I don't believe he is," said Janey, though the thought of "Maurice Hermann Sharcus" still troubled her now and then.

"We wondered if we should hide somewhere near here and follow him every night until we're sure," said Stefek.

"No!" Janey cried. "He'll be looking out for you now and if he catches you again he'll get you sent to a work camp for refugees. I know he will!"

Stefek looked puzzled.

"How do you know?" he asked.

"Because I heard him talking to Aunt Sarah one day, and she said the camps were awful places. No, you must go away and you must take care not to get caught."

"And let him go on spying?" said Stefek uneasily.

"Look," said Janey, "you'll just have to leave that to me. There's nothing else you can do. Now where will you go?"

"Well, we thought we could try to find the Polish army – or the air force. Tadek thinks the air force would be better just now, with all those planes coming over. There must be *something* we could do to help them."

Janey thought: "You're too young. They won't

want you." But she did not say that. Instead she said: "I'll go to the bathroom and bring a sponge so that you can wash your face."

Her own room was not close to the one where her aunt and uncle slept but she had to pass their door to get to the bathroom. She went very quietly, wondering what would happen if they came out and found her with a big wet soapy sponge in her hand and a towel over her arm. But the door stayed shut. Behind it she thought she could hear Uncle Maurice snoring.

"I'll give you some money," she said, when she was safely back in her own room. While Stefek tried to get rid of the soot she took a pound note from a box on the dressing-table. "That's all I have here," she told him, "but there's some more in my post office savings bank. My father left it for me."

"We'll pay you back some day," said Stefek, taking the money gratefully. "Thanks, Janey. There's just one more thing now."

"What's that?"

"Our gas masks. We ought to have them."

"So you should," she said. "I'll fetch them for you. Wait here."

When she came back, Stefek was fairly clean again, but there was a good deal of soot on the towel. Janey was not sure what she would do with it in the morning.

"I wish you could come too," Stefek was saying. "So does Tadek. We don't like leaving you here. Only they'd never take *you* in the Polish air force, would they?"

"No," said Janey sadly. "I don't suppose so. Yet when we were in France I fought the Germans just as well as you, didn't I?" She went to the window with him.

"We'll come back and see you as soon as we can," he promised as he climbed on to the roof and vanished into the darkness.

Janey stood there after he had gone, pressing her forehead against the glass. And suddenly she remembered that this was just how she had stood in the little French farmhouse on the night when Martin went away and left her there with the funny old woman. "You wouldn't be able to walk fast enough," he had told her. She seemed to hear his voice again – and Stefek's voice saying: "They'd never take *you* in the Polish air force." She felt angry.

Chapter 7

It was Tadek who woke first next morning. For a moment, as he felt the hard earth under his body and saw the sun shining through the leaves over his head, he thought he was in France again. Then he remembered. London, England. And Janey's uncle, the hateful Nazi. And the German bombers. And the Polish air squadron! He sat up suddenly. How were they going to find the Polish air squadron?

Tadek knew that there was now a Polish squadron in the Royal Air Force. He had read an article about it in one of the Shark's magazines and then he had seen a picture of Polish airmen in *The Times*. The picture showed the King and General Sikorski, the Polish commander-in-chief, inspecting the airmen at a Royal Air Force station where they were being trained, but unfortunately the newspaper did not say exactly where the station was. "In the Midlands" was all it told you.

Tadek understood very well why this description was so vague. The newspapers never gave information which might help the Germans. And people were not supposed to speak of such things either, if they happened to know. There were posters everywhere – on the walls, in shop windows, in buses and trains – warning people to watch their words in case enemy spies might hear them. "CARELESS TALK COSTS LIVES" one poster said. "WALLS HAVE EARS" said another.

The twins had been puzzled by this one. "It

37

means," Janey had explained, "that someone might be listening in behind a wall when you think there's no one there."

"There must be a lot of spies then," Tadek had said, imagining them creeping about behind walls everywhere. And it was at this point that he had first begun to wonder if the Shark might be one of them.

His brother Stefek stirred beside him now and murmured something in his sleep. Tadek leaned over and touched Stefek's arm.

"Wake up!" he said. "Wake up, Stefek! We'll never find the Polish air squadron if we just lie here!"

They walked through the park for a while, discussing what they might do, but they could think of only one plan that seemed worth trying. The idea came from Tadek: they would wander round London until they saw a Polish airman and then they would follow him.

"If we manage to trail him for long enough," Tadek said, "he'll lead us to his squadron. He's bound to."

The trouble with this plan was that there seemed to be no airmen at all on the streets that day, not even British ones. The twins wandered for hours without catching sight of a single airforce-blue uniform.

"Well, it's obvious," said Tadek gloomily. "All the airmen are waiting beside their planes, ready for the Germans when they come. We should have thought of that. They wouldn't be walking around uselessly like us, would they?"

Stefek looked gloomy, too, and did not reply.

By this time the boys had another problem: they were very hungry.

"I'm thirsty as well," said Tadek. "I wish it was like France, with lots of empty houses you could just go into and take things."

"You don't really wish that," Stefek told him firmly. "If it was like that here, it would mean that the Germans had come."

They began to look for a restaurant but they did not want to spend much money.

"I've heard about things called 'British Restaurants', you know," said Stefek. "They've been started specially because of the war and they're very, very cheap. Let's find one of those."

"We could ask a policeman," Tadek said without thinking. They both laughed.

In the end they found a British Restaurant in a street near Victoria Station and they bought sausages with chips and baked beans, then sponge pudding with jam and two big bottles of lemonade. It cost them a shilling each.*

"We can live for quite a long time on one pound," Stefek said when they came out. He made sure that he put the change safely in his pocket.

"If we just have one meal like that every day, we can live for ten days," said Tadek. "Surely we'll find the Polish air force before then."

They turned a corner and saw a soldier stepping into the street just in front of them, starting to cross the road. On the shoulder of his uniform there was a red flash, and on the red flash in white letters was the word: POLAND.

---

* One shilling is the same as five pence in the money we have today. In 1940 everything cost very much less than it does now, but the British Restaurants were cheaper than all the others.

The twins stopped walking and looked at one another.

"He'll do!" Stefek decided, answering the question that was in both minds. "What does it matter if we join the army instead? It's what we always meant to do anyway. Come on!"

It was easy to trail the solider because he was not at all suspicious. He turned left on the other side of the road, then right at the next corner. After that he crossed over again and turned left once more. The boys kept close behind. The soldier strode along briskly, never looking back.

"It's easy," said Stefek in Polish.

"It's a piece of cake!" Tadek agreed in English. He had learned what this meant a few days before. He was trying to learn as much English slang as possible.

"He's stopping," Stefek whispered. "Look!"

The soldier had slowed down outside a shop, he was turning into the doorway.

"What if there's a way out at the back?" said Tadek. "We might lose him!"

They ran forward till they could peer through the shop window.

It was a very small shop selling groceries and things like aspirin tablets and toothpaste and light bulbs.

"There won't be a back door," Stefek murmured. "It's all right."

Two posters were stuck on the window. One said: LEND TO DEFEND THE RIGHT TO BE FREE. The other showed a picture of a strong man with a spade and the words: DIG FOR VICTORY.

The twins looked through the space between the posters and they saw the soldier standing behind a fat woman in a flowery overall. He was waiting while she put things in her basket and gave her ration books to the shopkeeper.

"We haven't got our ration books," said Stefek. "It's just as well you don't need them in restaurants."

"You can buy *some* things without them," Tadek answered. But neither of them knew which things.

The woman turned round and the soldier tried to stand aside politely to let her pass, but there was very little space. Things were piled high round all the walls, leaving only a narrow path between the door and the counter. The soldier had to take care not to touch a shaky-looking tower of HP sauce bottles that stood on top of a box just beside him.

The woman came out into the sunshine with her shopping basket and smiled at the boys.

"You two nippers up to something, eh?" she said as she passed them. Then: "Lord love us!

Alike as two peas! Bless my soul! Can't think 'ow your mum tells one of you from the other!"

She walked away, cheerful and warmhearted, not knowing what she had done by reminding them of their mother.

They tried not to think of their mother usually. For when they did they had to imagine her either dead or in a German prison camp and they scarcely knew which was more terrible. So they did not dare to look at one another as the woman walked on down the street, humming to herself as if all the world was happy and at peace.

The soldier was buying something now. They couldn't see what it was but it was quite small, like a packet of razor blades maybe. The shopkeeper took his money and opened the till. A small white kitten jumped on to the counter and he stroked its back.

"He'll be coming out soon," Stefek said.

He wondered if they should move away from the window, wondered which way the soldier might go.

"Stefek!" said Tadek urgently. "Look to your right! There's a policeman!"

The policeman was only about twenty metres away but he did not seem to have noticed them. He was talking to a woman who had stopped him to ask something. He was turning, he was pointing along the street in the opposite direction.

Stefek's mind raced. The policeman mustn't see them together. Yet they mustn't run away or they would lose the soldier.

"Quick, Tadek! You go inside!" he whispered. "I'll follow the soldier. Then you follow me."

Tadek blinked, nodded, shot through the door – and bumped straight into the soldier, who was already on his way out.

"Przepraszam!" said the soldier (which means "Excuse me" in Polish).

"Przepraszam!" said Tadek almost at the same moment, without thinking. He stepped backward and his foot came down hard in the kitten's tail.

The kitten gave a wild little squeal. Tadek whirled round to see what had happened and his elbow knocked against the shaky-looking tower of HP sauce bottles. With a great crash, the tower toppled.

Then it was like skittles – one thing, as it fell, knocked over the next. the HP sauce bottles knocked over the bottles of Lyons coffee and chicory. The Lyons coffee and chicory bottles knocked over the packets of Kraft Velveeta cheese. The Kraft Velveeta cheese knocked over the packets of aspirin. The kitten squealed and the shopkeeper yelled. Tadek and the soldier began to try to pick everything up. Tadek was very red in the face and ashamed of himself.

Outside, Stefek hesitated, laughed and then ran in to help. As soon as the soldier saw him, he stopped what he was doing and he laughed too. Even the shopkeeper began to smile.

The twins were used to this. People always laughed when the second twin arrived without warning.

"Don't worry," said the shopkeeper, "it's not as bad as it looks." And surprisingly they found that only two of the bottles were broken.

The twins swept up the glass and wiped the HP sauce off the floor and the Velveeta cheese packets (though some of them stayed a bit smeary) and off the sides of the coffee and chicory bottles.

Then they told the shopkeeper that they were sorry. Stefek took some money out of his pocket and offered to pay for the damage, but the soldier stopped him.

"No, no," he said. "I will pay."

He did not speak English well but he struggled to say more: "No, it was my ..."

Then, as he tried to find the English word "fault", he suddenly remembered: this boy, the first one, had said a word to him in Polish! He gave up searching for the strange English word and he spoke swiftly in Polish instead:

"It was my fault as much as yours. I will pay."

He could tell at once that the twins understood him.

"So you are Polish boys?" he went on.

They nodded.

The soldier took out his wallet and gave the shopkeeper some money.

"Now," he said to the twins, "let's get out of here."

Chapter 8

The twins sat with the soldier at a table in a café where he had taken them and Stefek explained how they had reached England:

"We went through Yugoslavia, then we hid on a ship that was going to Marseilles. After that we travelled north through France, but the Germans invaded France too, so it was difficult. The next thing was we met an English girl called Janey and the three of us fought the Germans."

"Did you?" said the soldier. He did not sound as if he believed it.

"Yes, we did. Then in the end we met Janey's father, and we came with him in a little fishing-boat to England." Stefek paused. "That's *how* we came. *Why* we came was to go on fighting the Germans."

"That's how most of us came," said the soldier, paying no attention to Stefek's last sentence. "Are you hungry, boys? Do you want another biscuit?"

The twins took another biscuit and thanked him. Then he asked the question which they knew would come:

"What happened to your parents?"

It was Tadek who told him.

"Our father was in the cavalry and he was killed. He died charging against the German tanks. Our mother is missing. We do not know what happened to her. The Germans took her away."

45

The soldier made the sign of the cross.

"May God rest your brave father's soul and keep your dear mother in safety until you find her again," he said. "So you—"

The waitress came, bringing the bill.

"Are these your nippers, then?" she said, for she had heard them all speaking Polish.

"Excuse me?" said the soldier, not understanding.

" 'Nippers' means 'children'," Tadek explained. "She means, are we your children?"

"No!" said the waitress herself, looking more closely at the soldier. " 'Course they ain't. You're far too young. Not much above a boy yourself, are you?"

She collected the dirty cups and went away.

Stefek leaned across the table.

"So you see why we want to join the Polish army, don't you?" he asked very earnestly.

"Or the air force," Tadek added. He was just going to say: "That would be even better," when he remembered that he was talking to a soldier and thought it might not be very tactful.

Once again the soldier asked a question which had to come.

"How old are you, boys?" he said.

"Sixteen," Tadek told him quickly.

"Sixteen, eh?"

"Yes, sixteen."

But the soldier was shaking his head.

"You know, boys, they won't take you," he said gently. "It's no use. You're too young."

"Look," cried Tadek. "I know we're young, but there must be *something* we could do. Don't they have boy soldiers? Or cabin boys in the navy? Or *something*?"

But the soldier shook his head.

"We fought the Germans in France when we were all on our own, you know," Tadek went on. "We did really. We broke into their headquarters in St Quentin and we cut all their telephone wires. We made a lot of trouble for them. And now do you know what people would like to do with us here?" His voice grew louder and faster. "They'd like to send us to school! School! While there's a war like this going on! Well, we won't go to school! We'll go back to France, first! Right back to Poland even!"

He was shaking with excitement as he spoke, half standing up and leaning forward. People were turning to look, wondering what was wrong. The waitress whispered something to the café owner.

"All right, all right!" said the soldier. "Calm down!" He shoved back his chair. "Come on! I'll take you to the headquarters of the Polish army."

"General Sikorski's headquarters?" Tadek asked eagerly.

"That's right."

"Is it far?"

"Far? No. It's not far at all. It's in the Rubens Hotel in Buckingham Palace Road. Come on!"

Chapter 9

The recruiting officer at General Sikorski's headquarters agreed to see them. He was kind but quite firm. He understood very well their desire to fight the Germans and he thought it was a splendid thing. "Yes," he said, "a splendid thing. I'm proud of you."

However, he did not believe that they were sixteen, or even fifteen, or even fourteen. Twelve, maybe, at the most? Twelve at the most, in his opinion.

His eyes twinkled as if it was all a good joke which they could share. He stroked his thick brown moustache and looked at their smooth hairless cheeks.

"So you will have to wait a little," he told them. "But this war may last a very long time. Perhaps your chance will come."

Someone knocked at the door.

"Come in!" he called.

A soldier brought a telegram, clicked his heels together, saluted smartly and went away again. The recruiting officer opened the telegram, rose to his feet, said "Hmm! Hmm!" and walked over to the window, where he stood looking out as if he had forgotten that anyone else was there.

The boys were standing in front of the desk. Tadek noticed that there was a map on the wall, a few feet away to the right. It had flags stuck in it like the German maps in the headquarters at St Quentin. He moved quietly sideways, trying to see it better. He moved close, his heart beating faster. He began to scan the map, glancing to and fro between it and the recruiting officer's back.

The telephone rang, causing Tadek to jerk his head sharply to the front. The officer came back to the desk and picked up the receiver without seeming to notice that Tadek had moved. Tadek slid gently sideways again so that, when the telephone conversation had ended, he was standing next to his brother.

"Ah!" said the officer, raising his eyes and looking at them as if a magician had just caused them to appear out of the air. "Forgive me, so much is happening. Now you must go off home. You have been with an English family, you tell me. That is good. Go back there. Come to see me again when you are seventeen, but I mean *really* seventeen, remember! Off you go! The stairs are just along the corridor on the right."

Before they had time to leave the room the telephone had rung again and he had forgotten them.

"What did you see on that map?" Stefek said, as soon as they were outside.

Tadek's eyes gleamed.

"I saw where the Polish air squadron is stationed," he said. "It's called the Kosciuszko squadron. It's number 303 and it's at a place called Northolt just outside London. It's not in the Midlands at all. It's near here, Stefek! We can go!"

Stefek did not answer for a second. Then he said slowly: "You know what?" And there was something serious and sad in his voice which made Tadek stop where he was, at the top of the broad hotel stairway, and look round at him.

"What?" said Tadek.

49

"It's no good. They won't take us. We've been fooling ourselves."

Tadek looked down. There was a pattern of yellow flowers on the carpet, big yellow flowers on a blue background. He dug his right heel into the middle of one of them.

"Didn't you know?" said Stefek. "Didn't you really know, even before we came here? If we go to that place where the squadron is, we'll just be sick with wanting to get up in those Spitfires but they won't let us. They'll be kind to us, but we'll not be a help to them. We'll even be a nuisance, like we were to that man in there. We'll—"

"Oh, shut up, Stefek!" cried Tadek. "Shut up, will you?" And he ran quickly down the stairs into the entrance hall. Stefek followed him.

A soldier who was standing near the door smiled at them as they walked towards him.

"Here," he said, holding out his hand. "The man you came with had to go away, but he left this for you."

Stefek took the piece of paper which the soldier gave him. It was folded over in the middle. He opened it and read:

"If you ever need help, go to 126 Paradise Street in Bermondsey. Bermondsey is south of the river and east of Tower Bridge. You will find it quite easily. Say that Bogdan sent you. Good luck!"

Stefek folded the paper again and put it in his pocket.

"So what are we going to do now?" Tadek asked miserably.

"I don't know," Stefek replied.

"I wish we had stayed in Poland."

"So do I."

They wandered along, not even bothering to

keep a lookout for policemen.

"We could try to find our grandmother," Stefek suggested after a while. But they did not know her address, only that she lived near Southampton. Janey's father had put an advertisement in the paper to try to find her, but no one had replied.

"She'd only try to send us to school, anyway," said Tadek.

They came to the end of the street they were in and found themselves entering a much wider one.

"Look! There's the river," said Stefek suddenly, and they ran over. Below them was a jetty with several motor boats moored to it.

"Let's go down and look," Tadek suggested.

An old man came out of the cabin of one of the boats just as they reached it. His shirt sleeves were rolled up above his elbows, which seemed right in the warm afternoon. Yet round his neck he wore a thick woollen scarf with broad blue and green stripes. He waved to the boys and grinned at them.

"Is that your boat, sir?" Stefek asked him.

He nodded.

"She's my boat. The *Daisy Belle*." He looked at the boat lovingly but sadly. "Used to run 'er up and down the river all day long, packed with people. She just lies 'ere now. No petrol for pleasure trips no more and no people with time for 'em neither. On account of this 'ere war, you see. That German fellow, what's 'is name?"

"Hitler," said Stefek, "Adolf Hitler."

"Ah," said the old man, "but they do say that ain't 'is *real* name, don't they?"

"What's his real name, then?" Tadek asked.

"Schickelgruber!" said the old man. "That's what they say, leastways! Schickelgruber! Huh!"

He laughed and spat vigorously into the water.

Stefek remembered the Shark.

"Do you think we should stop fighting, then?" he asked. "So you can run your boat again, I mean?"

The old man got very excited.

"Stop fightin'? Not on your young life, sonny. Give 'im all we've got, I say – and that's plenty!"

He did a little dance from foot to foot, like a boxer. Then he looked around the *Daisy Belle* proudly and patted her side.

"She did 'er bit, my old Daisy, just the same," he said. "Took 'er over to France, I did, and fetched some of our lads off them beaches. Old she may be, but she went there and back, right to Dunkirk. You should've seen it. What a sight! All them little boats dotted about on the sea and the lads as thick as flies on the shore waitin' to get took off, and the dive-bombin' and machine-gunnin' all about us! See this?" He leaned over and pointed to some marks on the boat's side. "Bullet marks, see?"

He gave his scarf a tug to make sure it was good and tight. Then he eyed Stefek fiercely.

"Stop fightin'? Not likely! Wish I was younger, that's all. They won't take me in the army now, you know. Jake Fitchett's too old, they say!" He sighed, took out a pipe and began to fill it carefully.

The twins looked at one another.

"They won't take us either," Tadek told him. "They say *we*'re too young."

Old Jake stopped thrusting at the tobacco and looked up, interested.

"You've asked 'em then, 'ave you?" he said.

The boys nodded.

"We went to General Sikorski's headquarters and saw a recruiting officer, but it was no use," said Tadek.

"General *who*? That's a rum name!"

"Sikorski. He's the commander-in-chief of the Polish forces in Britain."

"Why go to 'im, then?"

"We're Polish."

"Never! English as they come! Look English, sound English."

Stefek said: "Our mother is English."

"Ah," said Jake, "that's it, then."

He was about to add something when Tadek suddenly asked:

"Could your boat sail to Poland?"

"To Poland, eh? I doubt that, lad. That's a long way. A long way, that is, through them cold north seas, thick with U-boats." He shook his head.

"Where's Ber – Bersand – *Bermondsey*, then?" Stefek asked.

"Bermondsey?" The old man began to laugh. He laughed so much that he had to hold on to the rail. "A lot nearer than Poland, I tell you that!"

When he had stopped laughing, he pointed eastward along the river.

"Along there, other side. You looking for someone in Bermondsey, then?"

"Yes. A Polish family."

"That's right. Plenty of 'em around there, I daresay. Well, good luck, lads. Come and see me again. Jake Fitchett, that's me. Mostly 'ere or 'ereabouts. Nothing much to do no more, that's old Jake Fitchett now."

Chapter 10

The children walked eastward till they came to Westminster where the hands of Big Ben were at ten past four.

"I bet the Germans would like to hit this with their bombs," said Tadek, gazing upwards.

"The Shark says they only want to hit airfields and things like that," said Stefek.

"I know," Tadek answered, "but I bet the Shark's wrong."

They crossed the bridge and continued on the far side.

"Are we going to Paradise Street?" Tadek asked.

They were walking as if they had a purpose, a place that they wanted to reach, but they had not spoken about it.

"It's a nice name," Stefek replied. "Let's take a look at it anyway."

They walked on in silence.

"I'm hungry again," said Tadek after a while, "but I don't suppose we can have another meal."

"No, we can't," Stefek replied firmly. "We have to make our money last as long as possible."

"What do we do when it's gone?"

Stefek shrugged his shoulders.

"We'll have to think of something. Perhaps someone will give us a job to do. We'll manage somehow. We always have till now, haven't we?"

"It seems harder here," said Tadek. "It was better in France."

By half-past five they were in dockland, among the long warehouses and the tall swinging cranes. There were ships to look at too, though not so many as in peacetime.

"Do you think one of these might be going to Poland?" Tadek wondered. "Do you think we should try to go home?"

"I'm not sure," said Stefek. "Let's find the Polish family in Paradise Street and see what they're like. Then we can ..." He stopped walking. "There it goes!" he said.

The air raid siren had begun to howl its warning. Everyone in the street looked up at the sky, but the sky was calm and clear, so no one hurried to take shelter. They were all used by now to air raid warnings when nothing much happened.

"Let's just walk on," said Stefek.

They walked on. But soon the sound of the planes began to reach them and the chatter of the guns from farther down the river.

Then they saw the bombers, a cluster of black dots to the east, growing larger. And they heard the first of the bombs falling, somewhere ahead. Suddenly it seemed impossible just to walk towards them. They stood still and looked at one another.

Around them now, the streets were emptying. They hesitated. There was no sign of a public air raid shelter and there was no air raid warden.

"You two nippers on your own?" said a voice behind them. "Better get 'ome quick."

"We can't do that," said Stefek.

The man who had spoken was small and fat and cheerful-looking. He was wearing dungarees and a cap so dirty that you could not tell what colour it once had been.

"Why not?" he asked.

"Our home's not near here," Tadek told him. It seemed the simplest thing to say.

"Right," said the man, "you want to take shelter then. This one ain't goin' to be no joke." He glanced over his shoulder. "This time they mean it," he said.

"Where can we go?" Stefek asked him.

"Tube station. Best place. Don't trust them surface shelters, not a bit. Death-traps, that's what they are!"

"I thought you weren't supposed to shelter in the Underground," said Tadek.

"You ain't, but who cares? Come on."

He led them at a quick trot back towards London Bridge then away from the river.

"In you go," he said, at the entrance to the station. "Ask for a ticket for three half-pence, that's the cheapest. They 'ave to let you in."

"Aren't you coming?" Tadek asked.

"Not me. Got to get 'ome."

He turned to go, then stopped.

"Got any money?"

"Yes, thank you," Stefek told him.

"On you go, then."

He smiled and hurried away.

Inside the entrance hall Stefek hesitated. He did not really want to spend money which they might badly need for food later on. But then he thought that it would not be much use to have money in your pocket if you were dead. He handed over three pennies and they went in and down.

They sat for two hours on the station platform, feeling safe but very bored, wondering how long it would last. Then someone shouted that the raid was over and all the people rose up at once and

57

headed for the stairs.

They did not push too hard, they were gentle with one another. They laughed and made jokes as they went up, thankful to be going out. But as each group reached the entrance hall they heard gasps and cries from those ahead of them and the jokes died away.

"What is it? What's happened?" they muttered instead. Then they, in their turn, pushed forward to the doorway and cried out at what they saw.

The whole world seemed to be ablaze. Spouts of flame rose high into the sky. Clouds of smoke, blue and black and grey and yellow, lay along the river and hung over the roofs that were not already burning. And the air was full of the strangest smells: bitter smells, sweet smells, sour smells, dark heavy choking smells.

"What is it?" Tadek cried, and a man beside him answered:

"They've hit the warehouses with fire bombs, sonny. You see, there's rum stored there and spices from the West Indies. And tea and sugar. And paint. And pepper. And rubber from South America. And they're all burning. Probably no one has ever smelt anything quite like this since the world began."

It was tempting to go underground again. The flames were very close, the fire might spread. People hesitated, half-turned. But the crowd behind was too dense and everyone inside was thrusting forward, wanting to see. There was no way back.

Suddenly someone shrieked, and pointed a finger at the sky. A block of wood, burning brightly, had been tossed into the air by an explosion in one of the warehouses. As the thing blazed like a rocket over the rooftops, Tadek followed its path with his eyes.

The sky was not yet dark but he saw the moon up there: a pale moon among the red and golden flames. He watched them curl and twist around it and, as he looked, its edges seemed to crumple and darken.

"Stefek," he said in a hushed voice, touching his brother"s arm, "I think the moon's on fire."

Chapter 11

The twins decided it was useless to try to get to
Paradise Street that day. The fires were burning
far too brightly all along the riverside. And in any
case people were pouring out of the district now.
It was hardly possible to stay there. The Polish
family would probably have gone away.

So the boys turned southward; and they were
still trailing wearily through the streets, wondering where they were going to spend the night,
when the bombers came back.

It was half-past eight on that Saturday evening
when the sirens sounded again to tell the people
that a night raid was coming. Only this one was
not like any night raid that there had ever been
before. For now, instead of the darkness of a
blacked-out land, there were flames waving
across the sky, like friendly arms guiding the
bombers in. From many miles away, while they
were still far out over the Channel, the German
pilots could see the heart of London.

"Where shall we go this time?" said Stefek. He
was a brave boy but his voice shook a little as he
spoke. They were both used to danger but they
had never known anything like this before.

"Another Underground station?" said Stefek.
But when they looked all around them they could
not see one and they could not remember having
passed one recently.

They were in an empty street where bombs had
fallen earlier. Several buildings lay in ruins or had

been partly destroyed. One of these was a tobacconist's shop. The door and the window had been blown out and some of the packets of cigarettes were lying about on the pavement among the broken glass.

"I wonder if there's a cellar," Stefek said. "Perhaps we could shelter there till this one's over."

They went inside and searched around. It was very dark but Tadek groped on the counter until his fingers reached a box of matches. Striking one, they found a trapdoor in the floor at the back of the shop and, below that, a flight of stone steps leading downwards.

"Good!" said Stefek. "That looks exactly right."

The cellar underneath was surprisingly large. Another match showed the boys that it was empty except for a few cartons which stood in one corner. Tadek went across and looked at them.

"Just cigarettes," he said, and he read the names aloud: "Gold Flake. Player's Navy Cut. Woodbine. But he hasn't really got very many left, has he?"

"Cigarettes are getting scarce now," said Stefek, "just like everything else. The ships can't bring them in easily any more because of the German submarines and the bombers."

"Listen to the bombers now," said Tadek. "They must be right over our heads."

The roar of the aeroplane engines was loud in their ears, even in the cellar.

"It's lucky that we found this place," said Tadek. And then the roof fell in.

They had not heard the bomb whining as it came down. Perhaps it had been floated down by parachute, as some were. But, more strangely, they did not even seem to hear the explosion.

61

They simply felt the earth shuddering and then the cellar crashed and crumbled around them.

When Tadek tried to move, he found that he was lying under a heap of dust and rubble. He thrust up out of it and discovered that a heavy wooden joist had come to rest a foot or so above his body. It had fallen against the wall in such a way as to shield him instead of crushing him to death. He wriggled out and sat up, coughing and sneezing because of the dust in his nostrils.

"Stefek!" he called as soon as he could speak, "Stefek, are you all right?"

There was no reply for a moment; then he thought he heard a faint groan.

"Stefek!" he cried. "Where are you?" And at the same time he reached into his pocket and found the box of matches. As he struck one, he heard the groaning sound again. And in the light of the match he saw Stefek's hand sticking up through the rubble about a foot away. He caught it and held if for a second.

"It's all right, Stefek!" he shouted. "I'll get you out. Don't worry!"

He had to move with great care to clear the dust and pieces of brick from Stefek's head and shoulders; but soon his fingers touched Stefek's hair and then his ear. A moment later Tadek had his arm round his brother's neck and was lifting him up.

"Stefek," he said, "can you hear me? Say something!"

Stefek's answer was a violent and reassuring sneeze. Tadek laughed with relief.

"You're all right then! Can you move?"

But Stefek shook his head.

"My leg," he said. "I think there's something on top of it, something heavy crushing it. It hurts badly when I try to move. And my back hurts, too."

Tadek saw then that the same big joist which had shielded him had pinned Stefek's right leg against the floor.

"I'll lift it," he said. "It won't take a minute."

And he seized hold of the joist and heaved. But it did not budge.

He heaved again. Then he tried to push the thing sideways. But he could not move it at all. It was wedged tightly where it lay, and he was not strong enough to shift it.

"I can't move it," he admitted at last. "I must get help."

But when he struck another match and turned towards the stairway he saw that it was blocked. He was going to have to dig his way out, through a great pile of wood and dust and broken bricks and plaster.

He set to work with his hands again, longing for a shovel and longing for light so that he could see what he was doing. Soon his fingers were torn and bleeding, but he scarcely noticed.

"I won't be long!" he shouted, tugging at a piece of wood. It came away, bringing a heap of rubble tumbling with it. He would have to be careful not to start a kind of avalanche.

He stood up, struck another match and was dismayed by what he saw. The end of a big steel girder was sticking out of the pile. He could never hope to shift that. The question was whether he could move all the other stuff without bringing the girder down upon him, and whether he could then somehow climb over it or round it to reach the trapdoor.

A new thought came to him then: had Stefek closed the trapdoor behind him as he came down? For if he had, and if there was more rubble on top of that, they might be trapped in this cellar for ever. Not a person in the world knew they were here.

Chapter 12

Tadek opened his mouth to ask Stefek about the trapdoor, then shut it again. Stefek was lying there in pain. There was no point in asking him worrying questions. The only thing to do was to keep on trying to get out.

"Tadek!" Stefek called.

"Yes?"

"You're not going to manage it, are you?"

"Of course I am."

Stefek was silent again. Tadek worked on.

The steel girder was proving to be a very bad problem. It lay right across the stairs in a most difficult way. And there seemed to be another wooden joist also, crossing over the girder higher up. Tadek longed to be twice as big and twice as strong. Also he longed once more for a better light to see by.

"Tadek!" Stefek called. His voice sounded weak and tired.

"Yes?"

"You'll never move that pile alone. Don't you think we should shout for help?"

"Who'll be there to hear us?" Tadek asked.

"Well, there might be a warden. They go round all the time, you know, looking for people who are hurt."

"We'll shout then," said Tadek. "But I'll go on working too."

They began to shout: "Help! Help!" But no voice came from above to answer them.

Tadek had another idea. He went back to Stefek's side.

"Could you sit up now," he said, "if I helped you? Then we could both try to move this thing from your leg. Perhaps if you shoved and I pulled, we could shift it."

Stefek managed to sit up though his back hurt badly when he did so. Then he tried to lift the joist from underneath while Tadek heaved at it from above, but still it was too much for them. Stefek lay down again, biting his lips so that he would not cry out with the pain.

"What was that?" said Tadek suddenly.

"What?"

"A noise! Up above! I think I heard a noise!"
Stefek managed to laugh.

"Another bomb maybe?" he said.

"Ssh!" cried Tadek. "A scrambling, scratching sort of noise. There's someone up there. Shout with me!"

So they shouted again: "Help! Help!"

The scratching noise stopped.

"Help! Help!" they yelled.

And this time a voice came back to them.

"OK!" it roared. "I'm coming!"

It was a loud and a deep voice, the voice of a powerful man. And then they heard a thudding and a scraping and a thumping.

The heap of rubble where Tadek had worked crumbled and fell apart, almost choking the boys with dust. The beam of a strong torch shone down on them.

"Come on up, then!" cried a voice from behind it.

"We can't!" said Tadek. "Well, at least I could, but my brother's stuck here. There's a big joist over his leg, pinning him down. We can't move it."

The voice grunted.

"Hold on, then!" it said.

"What a funny way he speaks," Tadek whispered. "Where do you think he comes from?"

Stefek did not know.

"From Heaven maybe," he said and smiled.

The light from the torch swept round the cellar.

"This is a right mess you kids have got yourselves into!" said the voice. "I'll come down, then."

He was a big man. The roof of the cellar was

high but he was too tall to stand upright in it. He leaned over Stefek, his broad shoulders hunched, and he looked at the way the joist was lying.

"Oh, aye," he said. "Here, you! Take a hold o' this torch."

While Tadek held it, the man bent and heaved, and the massive piece of wood came up as if it had been a matchstick. He tossed it to one side.

"Can ye move your leg now?" he asked.

Stefek tried and winced with the pain.

"Aye," said the man. He touched Stefek's ankle. "It's swollen real bad."

He took hold of the foot and moved it. Stefek cried out.

"But it's no' broken," said the man. "Ye'll be fine soon." He straightened up as far as he could.

"Give me that torch," he said, and shone it round the walls. "Was this place empty when you came in?"

"Except for some cartons of cigarettes," Tadek told him.

"Oh aye," said the man. "Where were they, then?"

"Over there. Look, you can see one of them sticking out."

"Uhuh," said the man. "Come on. I'll get ye out o' here."

He gave the torch back to Tadek. Then he lifted Stefek and carried him easily up the stairs while Tadek shone the torch to show him the way. There was still a great deal of rubble on the steps but there was no difficulty now in finding a path through it. Tadek followed them into the ruins of the shop and out into the street. Just as they reached the doorway they heard the All Clear.

Chapter 13

"Now," said the man, "what am I going to do with you two? Have ye a place to go?"

He stood there in the street still holding Stefek in his arms. All around them were ruined buildings and fires still blazing. There was a strong smell of gas in the air.

"Not really," Tadek admitted. "We were trying to get to Paradise Street when the first sirens went off. Then we couldn't go because of the fires."

"Is that your home, then, Paradise Street?"

"No," said Tadek.

"Hmph," said the man. "Have ye a home some place else, then?"

"Not really," said Tadek.

"Hmph," said the man.

For a moment they stood in silence.

"Oh, well," he said, "I'll take ye back to the Wolf's lair – if the place is still standing, that is. But ye canna stay long. OK? Ye get me?"

"OK," Tadek replied. "I get you. Thank you very much, sir." But he thought to himself: "What does he mean by 'the wolf's lair'?"

"Hmph," said the man.

A cart like the kind used for selling fruit in the streets was standing near the door. The man put Stefek down in it. Then he said:

"Er, just you two wait here a minute. OK?"

And he went again into the ruined building.

"What has he gone back in there for?" Stefek asked.

"Don't know," said Tadek. "Perhaps he left something behind."

"Why was he there in the first place? He's not a warden, is he?"

"No, he's certainly not a warden."

The man came out again, carrying two big boxes. As he put them down beside Stefek the twins saw that they were cartons of cigarettes.

"Is that your shop, then?" Stefek asked.

"Eh? Mine? No, it's no' mine. I just promised the man that owns it that I'd pick up his things for him, that's all. Help him out, like. He couldnae come for the stuff himsel', ye see, no' right now. I'll be back in a minute."

He moved quickly into the shop again.

"Do you believe him?" Tadek asked in a whisper.

Stefek shook his head.

"I don't think so," he said. "I think he's stealing them."

The man appeared with two more cartons.

"That's it, then," he said. "All safely gotten out. Off we go!"

As they reached the end of the street, two fire engines came racing along.

The man stopped to let them pass, then looked after them and began to sing in a deep voice:

"London's burning, London's burning,
 Fetch the engines, fetch the engines,
 Fire! Fire! Fire! Fire!
 Pour on water, pour on water!"

Tadek and Stefek remembered how their mother had taught them the same song, far away in the High Tatra mountains, long ago. But they wondered how this man could sing it at such a time.

The building where the man lived had not been damaged. He took them to an attic at the top of it, unlocked the door and switched on the light. Tadek followed him in and looked around.

The room was packed full, but not with furniture. There was a gas cooker, an old armchair and a kind of couch against one wall. The rest of the space was taken up by a collection of boxes and crates of many shapes and sizes. They were stacked everywhere, almost to the roof, in unsteady-looking piles.

Some of these crates were obviously used in place of the furniture that was missing. One of them had served as a table, for there were dirty cups and plates on it. And a lamp was balanced on top of three smaller boxes beside the gas fire.

The man put Stefek down on the couch, straightened up, and turned around. Then Tadek saw him clearly for the first time.

71

He had a broad face, with a big nose, wide nostrils and a wide mouth. His skin was pale and there were many large brown freckles scattered over it. The eyes were bright blue but half-hidden by heavy lids and by even heavier shaggy eyebrows. It was a strange face, fierce and wild.

The man stretched himself and yawned. Then he pulled off his cap and Tadek tried to choke back a gasp of surprise. For the face was young-looking, but the thick untidy hair which the cap had hidden was white.

He looked down at Tadek, his eyelids almost closed:

"What was that ye said?"

"Nothing, sir," said Tadek.

"Hmph," said the man. He crossed the room, opened one of the boxes and took a bottle from it. Then he lifted a cup from the table, looked inside it and, without washing it, filled it about half-full.

"That's better," he said, when he had taken a long gulp. "That's no' so bad!"

Chapter 14

Tadek sat on the couch beside his brother. The man slumped into the old armchair and looked as though he might fall asleep. But after a few minutes he opened one eye and muttered something.

"Excuse me, sir," said Tadek, "I didn't hear."

"Do ye want a cup o' tea laddie?" the man roared, in a sudden bellow that made Tadek jump.

"Yes, please."

"Help yoursel' then. There's a kettle there, see. And tea yonder. And cups lyin' around. Help yoursel'."

Tadek boiled a kettle, washed two very dirty cups and made a pot of tea. But as he poured it out he thought he must offer some to the man.

"Will you have some tea, sir?" he said.

"No, no. This is my tea here in the bottle. A wee dram, that's the tea for me."

"What's a wee dram?" said Stefek from the couch.

"Do ye not know that?" asked the man in a voice full of surprise. "I thought that even the English kids knew that much!" And he laughed.

"Are you not English, then?" said Tadek.

"English? Not me! Can ye no' tell I'm a Scot?"

"No, we couldn't tell," Stefek explained. "We're not English, either – at least only half. Our father was Polish."

"Do ye tell me that, now?" said the man. And

73

he sat up, looking interested, the fierce blue eyes wide open for the first time. "Half English! Well, that's better than whole English, anyway. Though maybe two halves make a whole, eh?" And he laughed as if he thought he had made a good joke.

"What are your names?" he asked suddenly a moment later.

"I'm Stefek Pulaski. He's Tadek."

"Funny like names," the man muttered.

This annoyed Tadek.

"What's *your* name, then?" he asked angrily.

"My name? I'm Wattie. Some call me Wattie the Wolf. Now why they call me that I wouldn't know."

He opened his wide mouth and grinned, showing a row of large, yellowish teeth.

"Wattie the Wolf!" he said, as if it pleased him. "Not the Wolf of Badenoch, mind you. Have ye heard o' him?"

He looked from one of them to the other. They shook their heads.

"Ignorant bairns!" he said. "Anyway, what does it matter. I'm no' the Wolf of Badenoch, I'm the Wolf of Maryhill!"

This seemed to be another joke for he laughed loudly.

"Where's Maryhill?" said Tadek.

Wattie shook his head sadly.

"In *Glasgow*," he cried. "Do they no' teach ye nothin' in Poland?"

Tadek was furious.

"Where's Zakopane?" he snapped.

Wattie opened his left eye wide and looked cunning.

"In Poland," he answered.

"That's not enough," said Tadek. "Where in

Poland?''

The eye closed again. Wattie took a big gulp of his drink. There was silence.

"You don't know, do you?" said Tadek. "Do they no' teach ye nothin' in Scotland?"

"Cheeky wee devil!" growled Wattie. "If I could be bothered, I'd let ye have a good skelpin'."

But it was obvious that he was not really angry. In fact he made a noise that might have been a chuckle. He began to fumble in his pockets and took out a cigarette packet. But it was empty.

"Nane left!" he said, and dropped it on the floor. "Oh, well, we're no' short o' them, luckily."

He got up, opened the carton with "Gold Flake" on the side, took out a packet and lit a cigarette.

"My friend'll no' mind if I have one o' these," he said with a grin.

"I think," said Tadek, "that I'd like to wash my brother's leg and bandage it, please. Have you got a piece of cloth I could use?"

"Bandage?" said Wattie. He looked round vaguely at the heaps of boxes. "There must be something in one o' these. Where would it be, now? Oh, aye! Try that one in the corner."

When Tadek opened the box he found that it was full of things which had obviously come from a chemist's shop. There was soap and talcum powder; there were bottles of cough mixture and bottles of perfume; there was face powder and lipstick; there were bottles of iodine; there was cottonwool and there were bandages.

He washed Stefek's leg and he put iodine on the places where the skin was broken. Then he began to bandage the ankle carefully. Wattie watched

him sleepily.

"How did you two kids end up in London?" he asked after a few minutes.

So while Tadek worked on the bandage he told Wattie the story.

At first Wattie looked as if he wasn't really listening. But when they came to the part where the twins were finding their way across France, he sat up suddenly.

"What did ye live on?" he asked. "What did ye eat?"

"At first, when we were in the South, people were kind to us," Tadek explained. "Sometimes they gave us jobs to do and paid us for them. Sometimes they gave us food to help us. But later, when we came to the parts in the North where the Germans were, it was difficult."

"What happened, then?"

"Well, the French people had all gone away. They had left their homes empty."

Tadek hesitated. He was beginning to feel embarrassed.

"Aye," said Wattie. "Go on."

"We went into the houses, and we ate any food that had been left behind."

"Just so," said Wattie. "And what else?"

"What else?"

"What else did ye take forbye food?"

Tadek flushed.

"What does 'forbye' mean?" he asked.

"You know fine what I'm askin' you," Wattie replied. "Maybe you never heard that word before but you know fine what I mean. What else did ye take?"

"Not much. Some tools once, but that was when we needed them to fight the Germans."

"Clothes?"

"Well, sometimes."

"Just so, You took what you needed, eh?"

He emptied the cup and poured another drink for himself from the bottle.

"I've just had a good idea," he said. "You can call it a brainwave. You two lads can work for me for a while."

The twins did not speak. Wattie frowned.

"Well," he said, "what's wrong with that? You've no place to go, have you? Nothin' else to do." He took a long drink. "Have you?" he asked aggressively.

"What do you want us to do?" said Stefek.

Wattie sat back more comfortably in his chair.

"Just help me, like," he said.

"But help you to do what?" Stefek persisted.

"Ah, well," said Wattie, "Here's how it is, to let you see. This world's no' a fair place. Some folk have more than they need, and some don't have enough. Now take me. I've never had quite

77

enough. So I'm trying to put that to rights, see?"

"You mean you're stealing things?" said Tadek.

"Oh, I wouldnae put it just like that," said Wattie. "A lot o' that stuff would have got wasted if I hadnae gone out and rescued it, wouldn't it now. A rescue operation, that's what it is. For the stuff—" he grinned, showing the yellow teeth "— and for me."

"I still think it's stealing," said Tadek.

"Oh, ye do, eh? Well, what was that you did in France, then, Snow-white?" Wattie asked, and his voice was sneering.

"That was different," Tadek told him.

"It's always different when it's something you want to do yoursel'," said Wattie.

For a moment they were all silent. Then Wattie spoke again.

"Look," he said, "I saved your lives, did I not? And I brought the pair o' you up here and I've given you bandages – stolen bandages, you'd say, but I see you've used them just the same. Now are you goin' to help me?"

Tadek and Stefek looked at one another.

"For if not," said Wattie – and his voice became deep and threatening – "I'll throw you out on the street, do you hear me?"

Tadek looked at his brother's pale and weary face.

"All right," he said quickly. "All right, we'll do what you say."

"We won't!" said Stefek, trying to sit up.

"*I* will!" said Tadek. "Lie down, Stefek. You can't do anything else."

He turned and faced the Wolf of Maryhill.

"Tell me what you want me to do," he said.

Chapter 15

While Tadek was struggling to clear away the rubbish that blocked the stairs in the tobacconist's cellar, Janey was standing by her window in the darkness, listening to the roar of the planes and watching the glow of flames in the sky.

This time she was really frightened. She wished that her dog Ghost was with her, not only because it would comfort her but because she knew he would be frightened too, if he could hear the bombs in that place where they were keeping him.

It was foolish not to be down in the cellar tonight, taking shelter there, she thought. But Uncle Maurice was such a stubborn man.

Then she heard Aunt Sarah's voice.

"Janey!" she called from just outside the door. "Janey, my dear!"

Janey closed the curtain quickly and turned round. Aunt Sarah was in the doorway, outlined against the light from the landing. She came into the room talking fast.

"Janey, we are all going down to the cellar. Your uncle has agreed that it's the best plan, though I'm sure there's nothing to worry about. Now put a warm coat on, there's a good girl! And socks and shoes. Even on a summer's night it's cold down there."

Janey nodded and bent to put her socks on. She could see that Aunt Sarah was shaking with fear though she was trying not to show it because she believed that grown-ups should always pretend to children that nothing was wrong.

"And yet," Janey thought, "I know more about war than Aunt Sarah does. I've actually been in a country where the Germans were and she hasn't."

"Are you two coming?" Uncle Maurice called from along the corridor.

He had a big torch in his hand in case the electricity should go off. He led the way downstairs.

"Mind you," he said, looking back over his shoulder, "I don't really believe this is necessary. If we let our whole lives be changed by the war, there's no telling where it will end. We'll all be living in caves again before long."

As they reached the hall, the windows at the front of the house rattled violently. Aunt Sarah jumped at the sound.

"There's nothing to worry about," said Uncle Maurice. "That noise is not important, you know. The blast from a bomb can make windows rattle from many miles away."

All the same he moved rather quickly across the hall to open the door that led to the cellar stairs.

"You go first this time, Sarah," he said. "I'll stay here and switch the light off when you're safely down."

The cellar stairway itself was not lit. Light reached it either from the hall above or from the cellar below.

Aunt Sarah nodded. She gathered her nightdress up from her ankles with trembling fingers and began to go down. But she had not taken more than two steps when the noise came:

a loud cracking noise, very sudden and very close. Aunt Sarah gave a little startled scream. Janey saw her body jerk upwards, then twist and tumble. She landed with a thud and a dreadful cry somewhere down in the darkness.

"Sarah!" cried Uncle Maurice. "Sarah! What's wrong?"

He pushed past Janey and switched on the torch.

"Why couldn't he have done that earlier?" Janey thought. In the beam of light she saw Aunt Sarah lying across the last few steps, with her head down and one foot sticking back up at a funny twisted angle. She seemed to be clutching her stomach and she was moaning.

Uncle Maurice rushed down and bent over her. There wasn't much room to move for the steps were narrow. She cried out again as he touched her. He climbed past her then and tried to move her by pulling at her shoulders. Janey ran to see if she could help.

"Yes, put your hands under her knees," Uncle Maurice gasped. "There! There!"

Aunt Sarah was moaning and trying to speak. All Janey could hear was "... the baby ... lose the baby." There were other words but they were too jumbled to make out.

They managed to drag her down on to the cellar floor where she could lie flat. But it was very hard and very cold. No one had arranged to have mattresses put there.

"I'll go and bring blankets," said Janey, "and an eiderdown or something."

She hurried away and came back a few minutes later with an armload of bedding.

Uncle Maurice met her at the foot of the cellar stairs.

"We need an ambulance," he said, "but she won't let me leave her."

His hair looked wild and untidy. Usually it was slicked back very smoothly. He put oily stuff called Brylcreem on it to keep it that way.

"I'll go," said Janey. "I'll call one."

She ran to the telephone in the hall and lifted the receiver, but when she tried to make a call nothing happened. She shook the instrument hard and tried again, but it was no use. A bomb must have hit the telephone exchange or brought the wires down somewhere.

She heard Uncle Maurice's voice as she turned back. He was halfway up the stairs, shouting down to Aunt Sarah:

"I'm not going away, Sarah. I'm here. Jane is telephoning for an ambulance."

"The telephone won't work," Janey whispered. "It's quite dead. A bomb must have done it."

"But it *must* work," Uncle Maurice whispered back. "We *must* get your aunt to hospital. She's very ill."

"I'll go out," said Janey. "I'll go out on to the street and I'll look for a taxi or someone with a car."

Uncle Maurice used to have a car but he had sold it a month ago. "What's the use of keeping this," he had said, "when there's scarcely any petrol to run it any more because of the war?"

Chapter 16

Janey ran out into the roadway, but it was quite empty: no taxi, no car, no people in sight. She looked around, wondering where to go.

"There won't be a taxi," she thought, "there won't be any cars. People won't take cars out in an air raid. What shall I do?"

She decided to go in the direction of the wider street which ran at right angles to the one where they lived. "Perhaps the air raid won't last much longer," she thought.

But there was really nothing to suggest that this might be true. Sometimes the sound of the aeroplane engines would fade away for a few moments as one wave of bombers turned and headed back towards the coast. But always there would be another wave coming in behind.*

Janey turned into the wider street and looked all around her, but she saw no one. Then suddenly she remembered that there was a post office farther along on the other side, and outside the post office there were two telephone boxes. It was just possible that one of them might still be working. She crossed the street and ran towards them. They were both empty.

Quickly she tried the first one, but the phone in it, like the one at home, was dead. There was very

---

* On that one night there were two hundred and forty seven German planes sent to bomb London.

little hope that the other would be different, she decided, but it was worth trying. Anything was worth trying.

She opened the door of the second box and put one foot inside. But before she could move the other foot after it she felt something brushing against her ankle and she heard a tiny yelp. Bending down, she felt warm fur under her hand. She picked up a small puppy, quivering with fear.

Janey was very angry. The puppy could not have got into the telephone box on its own because the door closed with a strong spring. Someone must have put it in there, someone who wanted to get rid of it. She rubbed its nose and it put out its tongue and licked her finger.

She did not hesitate then. She could not leave the animal there, it was quite impossible. What might happen later was another problem. Now she must take the puppy with her.

As she left the box she heard a car engine and she turned at once to wave, hoping it might stop. But it raced past her without slowing down.

She began to run again, then paused at the corner wondering which way to turn. And as she stopped running herself she became aware that there were feet behind her, heavy feet running after her.

She had been looking for someone to speak to, someone who might help. But now, hearing those feet, she was afraid. She glanced back, then ran again, as fast as she could go. A voice behind her yelled: "Hey, there! Stop!"

It was a big man, she was sure of that. He would be able to run much faster than she could. He would catch her if he wanted to, that was certain – unless she could hide.

Round the next corner she dashed into a shop

doorway and stood there breathless. He stopped at the corner and looked along the street. She could see his shape quite clearly.

He came slowly towards the doorway, puzzled by her disappearance. She drew right back into the darkest shadow — and the puppy squealed. The man swung round at once.

"Ha!" he said, and shone a thin beam of light in upon them. "There you are!"

Janey held the puppy tightly and longed for Ghost. If Ghost was here his hair would be standing out all round his body and his teeth would be bared, he would be growling and snarling, the man would be terrified. But Ghost wasn't here. She took a deep breath.

"Yes, I am," she said, "but it's none of your business. Go away, please."

"Oh, but it *is* my business, young lady," said the man. "It's very much my business to see that

85

children aren't running around alone in the middle of an air raid."

Then suddenly she noticed the tin hat on his head.

"You're a warden!" she cried.

He nodded. "That's right. Now what are you doing out here? Has your house been hit? Is that it? Are there people injured?"

But she shook her head.

"No, not that, it wasn't a bomb. It's my aunt. She's very ill and we tried to telephone but the phones aren't working and we need an ambulance. We need it very badly and I don't know where to go."

"An ambulance!" he said. "That won't be easy on a night like this, you know. Every ambulance in London is out, bringing in people from the places which have been worst hit — places like Stepney and Bermondsey. Still, I'll see what we can do."

He took out his notebook, put the torch in his pocket and switched on another little torch which hung round his neck.

"Now, what's wrong with your aunt?" he said.

Janey was not sure how to explain.

"I think ... I'm not sure," she said. "I think it's the baby."

"The baby?" said the warden. "You mean ..." He paused and frowned. "It's your *aunt* that's ill, is it?"

"My aunt. But I think she's going to have a baby," Janey told him. "And she fell on the stairs going down to the shelter, and ..."

"Ah," said the warden, "I see. Where's your uncle, then? Away in the army, is he?"

"Oh, no," said Janey. "He's in the shelter with her."

"You mean he let *you* come out all alone to look for help?" said the warden in a very disapproving voice.

Janey felt that this wasn't quite fair to Uncle Maurice.

"She didn't want him to leave her," she said.

"Hmm!" said the warden. "Well, I don't know. Anyway, you give me the address and I'll do all I can. If anyone can get you an ambulance tonight, I'm the man."

But it was nearly another hour before a taxi came to the door and took Aunt Sarah away.

Chapter 17

Tadek slept for many hours the next day. Stefek managed to doze now and then, but the pain of his leg kept waking him. While he was awake he watched Wattie and sometimes he saw that Wattie was watching him with a cunning look on his face. But they did not speak to one another.

Wattie did not seem to need sleep. He spent most of the day sitting in the armchair, smoking and drinking. Perhaps, like Stefek, he had an occasional brief nap but that was all. In the late afternoon he went out. As he left, Stefek heard a key turning in the lock and knew that they were prisoners.

Wattie looked pleased when he came back an hour later. He was carrying two loaves of bread.

"Wake up, laddie!" he roared. "We'll have our tea and then we'll get ready for work."

He produced a tin of corned beef from one of the boxes and began to open it.

"Put the kettle on, Snow-white!" he said.

"Don't call me that name!" said Tadek angrily.

Wattie was amused.

"Do ye no' like it? Well, that other name o' yours is too hard for me, so ye'll just need to put up with it."

They ate corned beef between thick slabs of bread and drank strong tea with lots of sugar in it.

"We've no ration books," said Tadek.

Wattie gave a roar of laughter.

"That'll no' matter to me," he said. "Ye're in luck, laddies!"

"Why are you not in the army?" Stefek asked.

Wattie grinned and winked.

"Oh," he said, "I've got a strange disease. Medically unfit, that's me."

"What's wrong with you?" said Stefek. And his voice showed that he did not believe there was anything wrong at all.

"I get funny dizzy turns," said Wattie. "Very funny. Just when I'd be goin' to fire a gun, like, I'd get all dizzy and it'd go off in the wrong direction. Might kill my own officer, as like as not! No use for the army. No use at all!"

He shook his head solemnly.

"I don't believe you," said Tadek. "You're very strong and you're quite young. You should be fighting like everyone else."

"Listen, Snow-white," said Wattie, "this is no' my fight. The folk that run this country are no' much bothered about what happens to Wattie the Wolf and I'm no' much bothered about what happens to them. It's mutual, see?"

He poured himself some more tea.

"I believe I'd just as soon have yon Hitler fellow," he muttered.

"You wouldn't if you knew," said Stefek.

When the meal was over, Tadek bathed Stefek's leg again. This time Wattie came to have a look at it. It was still badly swollen.

"We should get a doctor," Tadek said.

"No doctor here!" Wattie snapped. "It'll do fine. It's no' broken, I tell ye. Bandage it up again."

He wandered over to the window and looked at

the sky. It was beginning to darken.

"You're *hoping* the bombers will come again!" Tadek cried, with sudden understanding.

Wattie did not answer. But when, a little later, the air raid warning sounded again it was clear that Tadek had been right. Wattie had been slumped gloomily in the armchair. Now he sat up, leaned forward, put out his cigarette and looked brisk and pleased.

"Here they are, then!" he said. "We'll just give them a wee minute or two to get going. Then you and me'll get going too, Snow-white."

"We can't go out in a raid and leave Stefek all alone here!" Tadek cried.

"Oh, but that's just what we're going to do," Wattie told him. "And don't you give me any o' your cheek. See this fist?" He held up his big powerful right hand. "If I hit you with this, you'll waken up in the middle o' next week – or maybe you'll no' waken up at all. So just you do what I tell ye. OK?"

"Do what he tells you," said Stefek in an anxious voice.

The firemen had been working all day to put out the fires from last night's raid and they had managed to get them under control. But now it was all starting again. As Tadek walked through the streets by the Wolf's side he saw the flames beginning to leap into the sky once more. And, once more, the worst of the bombing was in places near the river.

"It's the docks they're after, and no mistake," said Wattie. "I was hoping we could maybe get in to some o' the warehouses there, if the bombers went some place else tonight. But no such luck. So we'll just need to settle for a shop or two."

Wattie had several sacks with him tonight instead of the barrow.

"Yon barrow's maybe a wee thing obvious," he said.

Tadek thought the sacks would be just as obvious once they were full, but he said nothing.

There was a brief silence, with no planes to be heard, and no bombs falling, only the crackle of the broken glass under their feet where it still lay thick from the night before. Then a gun sounded down the river and the throb of engines reached them again.

"Coming right for us!" Wattie muttered. "You just lie down and cover your head if they get real close, OK? Ye're as safe out here as in the shelters, maybe safer."

Tadek did not reply. He was wondering what would happen if they met a warden and whether he could risk telling him about Stefek and asking for help. But what if the warden was too busy and couldn't come for a long time? The Wolf would be furious and there was no way to tell what he might do. Tadek decided it was too dangerous.

"Down!" Wattie yelled in his ear. "Down, laddie! Mind the glass!"

They threw themselves down in the roadway among the splinters as the stick of bombs fell. Three explosions sounded one after the other. Then there was a short gap followed by a fourth bang.

Wattie got up on his knees and let out a long sigh.

"One o' them didnae go off," he said. "That's bad. That means an unexploded bomb somewhere round about here. And I don't fancy comin' on that while we're working."

"Why do you want me to help you?" said Tadek, brushing glass off his trousers. "Why does a big man like you need help from someone like me?"

"Use your loaf, son!" said Wattie.

"What?" said Tadek. "My loaf?"

Wattie tapped him on the head.

"Your loaf. Your head. Your brains, laddie. You can crawl through wee holes – holes that are far too wee for me. We'll make a grand team, the two o' us!"

Tadek said nothing. But he thought to himself: "No, we won't. Watch out, Wolf! I'm going to find a way to stop you." And he thought: "If only Stefek could walk again!"

Chapter 18

Wattie and Tadek turned left and found themselves in a wider street.

"There's some good shops here," said Wattie. "We might be lucky."

Then suddenly he grabbed Tadek by the arm and pulled him into a doorway.

"Ssh!" he said. "I think the warden's coming. Not a word now!"

Tadek had not heard footsteps. But Wattie was right. A moment later Tadek saw a little figure with a tin hat on its head going past them on the other side of the road.

"What a small man!" Tadek whispered.

"It's no' a man, it's a woman," said the Wolf. "I know her fine. This is her patch we're in and she's a fearsome woman. She scares me, I tell you. She's away, though. We're all right. Come on!"

At the end of the block they found a grocer's shop with a big hole blown in the side wall. They climbed in.

"Tins o' meat," said Wattie, "that's what we want. Or fish." He flicked on his torch for a second. "John West's Middle Cut Salmon. That's great. And here's some ham. Just the job. Now you fill this sack, Snow-white. Get cracking!"

The planes were above them again now. This time they heard no explosions but when they looked through the shop windows they saw that a new fire had started only a short distance away.

"Isn't that where your flat is?" Tadek

whispered, with fear making his stomach twist.

"Aye," Wattie growled anxiously. "It's over that way, right enough."

"What will Stefek do if the place is on fire?" Tadek cried. "He's helpless! It was awful to leave him there."

"Oh," said Wattie, "I'm no' bothered about him." And he actually laughed. Tadek hated him then.

"I have to get back!" he yelled, and he ran without picking up his sack. So Wattie had to take both sacks and lumber behind with them.

The heavy load was enough to stop him from overtaking Tadek, but only just. They stopped at almost the same time in front of the building where Wattie had his attic. It was not burning. The flames were two streets farther away.

Wattie was breathing hard. He dropped the sacks, grabbed Tadek in both hands, lifted him in the air and shook him hard. Then he let him fall again and kicked him as he lay on the ground.

"Ye'll no' do that again, d'ye hear me?" he roared. "Ye'll no' run off and leave the job half done! Ye'll no' stop work till I tell ye!"

Tadek got slowly to his feet and backed away.

"Come on!" said Wattie in a quieter voice, "We're goin' in."

When they reached the attic, he thrust Tadek in just before he came in himself. Once inside, he locked the door and put the key in his pocket.

Tadek turned to speak to Stefek, then he stood staring while his face went pale. The couch was empty. Stefek was no longer there.

"Where's Stefek?" Tadek cried. "What have you done with him?"

"He's safe enough," said Wattie with that

yellow-toothed grin of his. "Did I no' tell ye there was no need to worry about him?"

"Where is he?" Tadek cried again. "Tell me!"

"No, I'll no' do that," Wattie answered. He was getting his bottle out as usual. "Ye see, I'm no' daft. I know fine you'd tell the police about me if you got half a chance. You'd bring them nosin' around here in no time if you dared. And that would put a stop to the activities o' the Wolf of Maryhill for some time to come. So it's no' goin' to happen, see?"

He took a long drink and settled into the chair.

"Ye'll no' do a thing if you're worried about what might happen to that precious brother o' yours, will you now? Very commendable, too! Brotherly love!"

He made a funny noise deep in his throat and spat into the fireplace.

"You've no need to worry," he said. "He's in a safe place, safer than this place, ye could say. And nobody'll harm him, just as long as you do what I tell you. Now, make yourself a cup o' tea or something and shut up, will you?"

He lay back in the chair and closed his eyes.

Chapter 19

Wattie made Tadek go out with him every night except Tuesday. That night they stayed at home and men came with a van and took some of the boxes away.

Then on Wednesday night Wattie made a haul which seemed to please him at the time: two cases of whisky. But on Thursday morning he was restless.

"How long are you going to keep me like this without telling me what's happened to my brother?" Tadek asked him as he lay slumped in his chair.

"Just as long as it suits me," said Wattie. "Now shut up, Snow-white. I'm thinking."

Tadek sat down on a box and thought too. He wondered again if there was any way that he could get a message to that warden, the little woman. "She's a fearsome woman," the Wolf had said. "She scares me, I tell you." So perhaps, if she knew what was going on she would find a way to help. But it was very risky. He sighed.

"Stop that din!" said Wattie. "Why do ye no' go to sleep?"

He rose and stretched himself.

"I think I'll away out," he said. "I've got some things to see to."

"What are you going to do?" Tadek asked.

Wattie looked surprised.

"What makes ye think I'd tell you?"

"Well," said Tadek, "I'm supposed to be your

partner, am I not?"

Wattie burst out laughing.

"Partner, eh? That's a good one! More like my slave, are ye no'?"

But he stopped at the door and looked back.

"Right, partner!" he said. "I'll tell you. All this is just a wee bit too slow for me. A case o' whisky here and a box or two o' fags there. Fine and dandy but slow. At this rate the war'll be over and the Wolf of Maryhill will still be nothing better than a scaffie. So what we're doing now is we're movin' into the big time."

He closed the door behind him and turned the key in the lock. Tadek sat wondering what a "scaffie" was and what Wattie meant by "the big time". He heard Wattie whistling as he went downstairs.

They went out that night as usual, with no sign at first of any change in Wattie's plans. When Tadek asked about a "scaffie" and about "the big time", Wattie explained that a scaffie was a scavenger – someone who picked up rubbish from the streets. But he wouldn't explain "the big time", he just said that was easy to understand if you used your loaf. "And anyway," he said, "you'll soon see."

Tadek did begin to see that something was different when Wattie went straight past several bombed out shops without even stopping to look at them.

"Where are we going?" he asked.

"To the docks," said Wattie. "Now hold your tongue."

That night there did not seem to be as many planes as usual and the sky was quiet for long stretches of time, though the All Clear had not

sounded.

Tadek was used to walking through bombed streets by now, but as he and Wattie came closer to the river he saw that the damage which had been done was growing worse and worse. They passed a building where the whole front wall had fallen outwards so that you could see into all the rooms as if it was a doll's house. A doll's house for a giant, Tadek thought.

They came at last to a long dark warehouse on the quayside.

"Here we are, then," said Wattie in a pleased voice. "We'll just take a good close look now."

They walked all the way round the building and Tadek was surprised to discover that it did not seem to have been bombed.

"But it hasn't been hit," he said.

"You're right, laddie," Wattie replied. "The thing is I'm just a bit tired of waiting for these Germans to hit the right places, see? Look over there!"

Tadek looked in the direction where Wattie

pointed and was just able to make out the hull of a large ship moored against the quay.

"Yon's the *San Domingo*," said Wattie, "and it's new in from Portugal with a rare load of stuff, I tell you that. The stuff's goin' into the warehouse tomorrow. They'll no' want to leave it there long of course, for it's too dangerous with all these bombs." He laughed. "But they'll no' need to worry. I'll get it out for them quick enough."

Tadek asked: "What kind of cargo is it?" But Wattie would not tell him.

"Just you wait and see," he said.

On the way home they raided a chemist's shop, but someone else had been there before them.

"See what I mean?" said Wattie. "This is gettin' hopeless. There's no' much left but toilet rolls!"

Tadek did not answer. He was thinking hard about something else.

Chapter 20

"Why are you keeping me here?" said Stefek. "How long are you going to keep me? Please tell me."

The woman who was bathing his leg did not answer his questions. Instead she said:

"Your leg's better, ain't it, sonny? The swelling's down. It'll soon be fine."

"Why won't you tell me anything?" Stefek insisted.

She pushed her dark hair back from her face and stood up. He could see that his questions troubled her.

"Because I can't, kid," she said. "That's why."

"Are you afraid of the Wolf? Is that it?"

She laughed, but it was nervous laughter.

"The Wolf?"

"The man who had me brought here. Wattie the Wolf. He must have given orders to those others, the two who came and tied me up and carried me here. He must have done. Don't you know him?"

"Look, sonny," she said, "I ain't goin' to tell you nothin' so you might just as well give up, see? You're bein' looked after all right, ain't you?" She began to put on the bandage again. Her fingers were gentle and skilful. "Well nursed, ain't you? So what are you goin' on about?"

"Where's my brother?"

She stopped and turned to him. She was surprised.

"Your brother?"

"My *twin* brother. Don't you know about him?"

"No, I don't," she admitted. She frowned and bit her lip and went back to her job of winding the bandage.

The sun came out from behind a cloud and shone on them through the dirty window. It was surprising that the glass in the panes had escaped the bomb blast so far.

In the sunlight Stefek saw that the woman's hair looked dry and dusty. The whole of London was dusty now because of the bombs.

She fastened the safety pin and stood up.

"Blimey!" she said. "It's 'ot, ain't it?"

She wiped the sweat from her forehead and Stefek saw the dark marks on her dress where she had been sweating under her arms.

"Couldn't I have a book to read or something?" he asked. "It's very boring to lie here alone all day."

"Boring!" she cried. "There's Moaning Minnie yellin' in our ears day after day and night after night and 'e says 'e's bored! I wish I was bored instead of dead scared!"

Stefek realised that "Moaning Minnie" was what she called the air raid siren.

He looked at the woman and he saw that, though her cheeks were plump and smooth, her eyes were tired and frightened. She turned to go.

"But could I have a book, please?" he asked again.

"Ain't got no book to give you," she told him and went away.

After she had gone Stefek stood up. He had tried standing the day before and had found that he

could do it without much pain. Now he was able to walk quite easily. He wondered if the woman guessed that he could. He crossed over to the window and peered through the small dusty panes.

Since it was late afternoon and the sun was shining in, he knew that he was looking westward. The room was one storey up in a narrow little back street. The wall on the opposite side had no windows, it was just blank grimy brickwork. A tall chimney farther along made Stefek think that it must be the side wall of a factory.

The street was empty, so far as he could see. He tried to open the window but it was stuck fast. It did not look as if it had been opened for years.

For the last few nights he had been left in this room alone during the raids. He guessed that the other people in the house went off to a shelter and he was sure that the woman did not like leaving him behind. Would they still leave him, he wondered, now that his leg was getting better? For tonight, if they did ...

He looked again at the window. Even if the glass was broken, the panes were so small that he would not be able to get through without breaking the wood. But he would manage to break that somehow. He scanned the room looking for a tool.

There was very little furniture, just the bed he had lain on, an old trunk and one small table. But perhaps the table would do to smash the window, woodwork and all, if he swung hard. And what then? Could he reach the ground? He would not dare to jump with his damaged ankle, but there must be a way.

He lay down on the bed and thought hard and waited for the night to come.

Chapter 21

Janey threw a stick for the puppy but he did not seem to know that he was supposed to run after it. Yet he seemed to be a Labrador. He had smooth golden hair and big feet. Janey looked at him and hoped that Ghost would not be jealous when he came back from the quarantine place.

She could hear Aunt Hilda calling so she lifted the puppy and went into the kitchen.

"Help me with this tray, child," said Aunt Hilda. "And wash your hands first if you've been playing with that dog."

Janey knew already that Aunt Hilda did not like the puppy. Aunt Hilda had arrived on Sunday, the day after Aunt Sarah was taken to hospital. She was older than her brother Maurice and fatter than him. She was bad-tempered most of the time.

"I've got far too much to do, you know," said Aunt Hilda as Janey washed her hands. "It's quite dreadful having no servants except old Mrs Cooper in the mornings."

Janey put three cups and saucers on the tray. She added a jug of milk and looked around for the sugar bowl.

"There's no sugar left. The ration's finished," said Aunt Hilda sternly. "We're all going to starve, it seems, before this war is over." She glared at the puppy as if it was entirely his fault that the sugar bowl was empty.

"It's quite absurd to keep animals at a time like this," she said, "when there's not enough food for human beings."

"Oh, but he eats very little!" Janey cried. This was not wise, because Aunt Hilda did not think that children should argue with her.

"The creature is getting bigger every day," she said. "He will be disgustingly large and greedy in no time at all. And he is a great nuisance, what's more, and very dirty."

Janey knew that Aunt Hilda was thinking of the messes which the puppy made on the floor. She thought of pointing out that this would soon stop when he was house-trained but she decided to say nothing. The best plan would be just to try to get him trained as quickly as possible.

She had to admit, however, that there was no way to stop the puppy from needing more food. And suddenly she felt very frightened, for she understood that Aunt Hilda thought he should be killed.

"Take the tray upstairs, Jane," said Aunt Hilda. "I'm almost too tired to lift it. It's all very well for you young people. You may be able to sleep in a cellar with bombs falling all around you but I

105

can't. And after the last four nights I really don't know how I'm going to carry on."

Janey did as she was told. She walked quietly and calmly upstairs. She sat quietly and calmly while Aunt Hilda poured the tea. But there was no quiet or calm inside here, and when she tried to drink her tea she found it was impossible. She put the cup down again.

"What's wrong with you, Jane?" asked Aunt Hilda sharply.

"I'm sorry but I don't want any tea today," Janey replied.

"Drink your tea, Jane!" said Uncle Maurice. "Your aunt has come to look after you. It's very kind of her and you should try to show that you appreciate it, you know. Drink your tea!"

"I *can't* drink it, I'll be sick!" Janey cried. She got up and ran from the room.

"Dear me!" said Uncle Maurice. "She's really a very emotional child. What do you suppose is wrong with her?"

"I know what's wrong with her," Hilda told him. "It's because I said we ought not to be keeping that stray dog she found. She is absurdly attached to the creature already. But we really must have him put down. I can't think why you let her keep him in the first place."

"She came back with him the night Sarah fell downstairs and I had other things to worry about, that's why," said Maurice.

"She's a difficult child in some ways. Seems to make a habit of finding stray dogs. She found one in France, I gather, and wouldn't leave him there. That one's in quarantine now and she can't wait to get him out."

"That settles it, then," said Aunt Hilda. "If she makes a habit of it, that's worse than ever. This puppy must go if I am to stay."

Her brother moved in his chair and looked worried.

"It will upset her badly, you know. And she has had a good many things to upset her recently. Couldn't we—?"

"I'm sorry, Maurice," said Hilda. "We've all had a good many things to upset us recently, haven't we? It's not easy for a woman of my age to leave her home in the country and come here in the middle of all this dreadful bombing. That puppy is the last straw."

Maurice sighed. "All right, Hilda," he said. "If you insist. But I don't want Sarah to hear about this until she's out of hospital and a little stronger again. Be careful not to speak about it when you visit her."

"I am not stupid, Maurice," Hilda assured him. "Of course, I won't. But we must see that Jane is not allowed to visit her. When will you have the dog taken away?"

"I'll have it done tomorrow," her brother replied. "The sooner the better now that we've made up our minds."

Janey sat by her window and wondered if she should take the puppy and run away. But if she went, where could she go? And when should she do it?

"Tomorrow is Friday the 13th," she thought. "That's not a lucky day."

Chapter 22

Early on Friday morning old Jake Fitchett stood on the deck of the *Daisy Belle* looking east along the river, and he talked to his boat as he often did:

"They've gone again, Daisy girl, and they ain't got us yet. Still bobbin' about on the old river we are, in spite of 'em."

He tugged at his scarf to make sure it was snugly settled round his neck. Then he took out his pipe, lit it, and puffed smoke into the quiet air, as if there wasn't enough smoke there already.

"Not so bad last night, was it, eh?" he said. "Not so many as usual. I reckon them boys of ours is shootin' 'em down so fast now that we'll soon be quit of 'em. We'll show that Schickelgruber fellow, you'll see!"

He puffed at the pipe again, sending out a small round cloud like an Indian smoke signal. Then he screwed up his eyes and stared at a figure that was coming down the steps to his jetty.

"'Allo!" he said. "Who's 'ere?"

It was a boy of about twelve, he supposed. The lad looked dirty and weary and he was limping badly.

"I've seen this kid somewhere before," Jake Fitchett thought. And just as he did so the boy spoke.

"You're Mr Fitchett, aren't you?" he said.

Then Jake remembered.

"And you're one o' them Polish boys that came

asking for Bermondsey, ain't you?" he said. He looked at the boy's clothes.

"You got to Bermondsey, then, did you, sonny? It was real bad along there, wasn't it? Where's your brother?"

"I don't know," said the boy. "I can't find him."

Jake Fitchett could see that the lad was worn out. As he stood there, he swayed a little from side to side, as if it was hard for him to stand upright. His face was pale under the streaks of dirt, his clothes were torn in several places.

Jake knocked out his pipe and put it away in his pocket.

"Come on board the *Daisy Belle*, son," he said. "Come and put that foot up for a bit and tell me all about it."

Thankfully Stefek took the hand that reached out for him. Then he followed Jake into the tiny cabin.

Jake got breakfast ready while he listened to Stefek's story.

"How old a fellow is this Wattie?" he asked.

"Not *very* old," said Stefek. "Maybe twenty-five or thirty, I think."

"Why ain't 'e in the army, then?"

"He said he had a strange disease."

"Strange disease!" cried Jake angrily. He put bread in the pan to fry it, along with the single egg which was there already. "Well," he said, "maybe it *is* a strange disease you 'ave if you go stealing from people who've just been bombed out."

He stuck a fork fiercely into the bread as if it had been Wattie himself and turned it over.

"Go on, then," he said. "Tell me the rest of the

109

story."

"Well," said Stefek, "last night when the air raid warning came again I waited a bit until there were some planes near and I smashed the window. Then I took a sharp bit of the glass and I used it to cut my blanket into strips. That made a rope for me."

"Good lad!" said Jake. "Go on!"

"I took the table and I used it to smash the woodwork of the window, because the panes were too small to let me through, you see. Then I pulled the bed across the room and tied my rope of blankets to the end of it. And I climbed down. It was really quite easy."

Jake put the egg and most of the fried bread on Stefek's plate.

"Eat up now," he said.

"Are you not having an egg?" Stefek asked.

"No, no," said Jake. "Don't want one."

Stefek hesitated. He was very hungry but he was also worried.

"Are you sure you're not giving me the only egg you've got?" he asked.

"Course I'm sure!" said Jake. "Now you eat up and no more nonsense. Old men don't get so 'ungry no more, not like young uns. Eat up and get on with that story."

Stefek thought he had never tasted anything so good as that egg and the fried bread.

"Well, what happened next didn't work out so well," he explained. "I tried to get back to Wattie's flat so as to find my brother, but I didn't know where the place was. I never knew the name of the street, you see. I thought maybe I'd recognise it if I just hunted around, for I knew they hadn't taken me far. But I couldn't find it. I wandered about all night and maybe I was close

to it, maybe I was *in* it, even. They all looked the same to me. I didn't know what to do."

"Then you thought of old Jake Fitchett, eh?" said Jake. "Is that it?"

Stefek looked slightly embarrassed.

"Well, not at first," he said. "Not till I came near here and saw your boat again."

"So where were you off to, then?" Jake asked.

"I was thinking of going to see a friend of mine. She's called Janey."

"Oho!" said Jake. "Now who's Janey?"

"She's a girl we met in France. And her

father's English, but she's living with her uncle and he's not a nice man. Actually my brother and I were living there too, but we thought her uncle was a spy and he found out that we were watching him and following him and there was an awful row. So we had to leave."

"What made you think your friend's uncle was a spy?" Jake asked.

"He thinks England shouldn't be in the war. He thinks we should make peace with Hitler."

"Huh!" said Jake. "Does 'e now? You''re well away from 'im, then!"

"Yes, but Janey's still there," said Stefek, "and I want to see her again."

"You should rest up a bit first," Jake told him. "You ain't in no fit state to do no more right now. Tell you what ..."

He paused and looked thoughtful while he lit his pipe again. Then he went on:

"You rest 'ere today till you feel a bit better, and I'll go and talk to some of me old pals and see what I can find out about this Wattie. If 'e' s been around on the banks of this river for any time at all, some of them are bound to know 'im. Then we'll see what we can figure out to get that brother o' yours back safe and sound. And you can go and visit Janey too. Will that do, eh?"

Behind the thick smoke, Jake's eyes were twinkling. He was delighted at the thought of having something to do again, something that was useful to somebody.

Stefek thanked him.

"You'll be all right 'ere on the *Daisy Belle*," said Jake. "Just you curl up on that bunk while I'm off to see what's doing. Big fellow you said? White curly 'air and yellow teeth, eh? We'll find 'im, son! You'll see!"

Chapter 23

At breakfast on Friday morning, Janey could feel that something was in the air, something was happening.

Breakfast was always a difficult meal because you were not supposed to speak. Uncle Maurice read *The Times* at breakfast and he did not like to be interrupted. So this morning when no one spoke to anyone else it was just the same as usual, on the surface. But underneath it was different. Janey knew.

Once when she looked up she saw Uncle Maurice watching her over the top of his newspaper. He raised the paper quickly to hide his eyes but it was too late: she had seen them. And Aunt Hilda was sitting in her chair even more stiffly and uncomfortably than usual. Janey knew. Friday the 13th, she thought.

"Well, I'll be off then," said Uncle Maurice, laying down his newspaper. "Off to work!"

He sounded as though he was trying very hard to be brisk and cheerful. Aunt Hilda looked up at him as he passed her and he gave her a slight nod as if to say: "Don't worry, I haven't forgotten."

Janey stood by the window and watched him as he went down the path with his rolled umbrella over his arm. The Shark ... A small one, but then some of the most deadly sharks are small.

"Come along, child!" said Aunt Hilda. "Don't just stand there! Help me to clear these dishes away."

Janey washed the dishes and dried them. When she had finished she said:

"Please, Aunt Hilda, I'd like to take the puppy for a walk in the park."

"No!" said Aunt Hilda sharply. Then she added in a quieter voice. "I want you to dust the drawing-room. Mrs Cooper has enough to do in the kitchen today to keep her busy. Also the silver needs polishing. There's a great deal of work to do in a house like this, you know, and the bombs are no excuse for laziness and carelessness. We have to keep our standards as high as ever. Off you go now, Jane. Do your work thoroughly."

Janey took a duster and went slowly upstairs. Inside the drawing-room she stood still for a moment thinking. Then she crossed over to the window.

She reached it just in time to see a van coming slowly along the street. The driver was glancing at the houses as if he was looking for one house in particular. On the side of the van, Janey read the words:

S. PERKINS
DOG KENNELS
VETERINARY SERVICES

She dropped the duster and ran.

When Mr Sharcus came home at lunch-time he was expecting trouble and he was upset by the prospect of having to deal with it. He liked to lead a quiet and well-ordered life. "I expect she'll be crying and sobbing and refusing to take her food," he thought.

The house seemed very quiet when he came into the hall. "She'll be in her room, refusing to come out," he said to himself. He put his umbrella in the stand, took off his hat and laid it down in exactly the spot where he always placed it. Then he looked in the mirror and smoothed his hair. And in the mirror he saw that Hilda had come silently up behind him and was watching him.

"Good heavens, Hilda!" he cried as he spun round angrily. "What a start you gave me! Is something wrong?"

"She must have known what was going to happen," said Hilda. "She has taken the dog with her, and I think she has run away."

Chapter 24

When Jake Fitchett decided to find out about Wattie the Wolf there were many old friends that he could ask, for he had lived on the banks of the river Thames all his life and he had worked on the river since he was twelve years old.

Each visit to one of his friends tended to last a long time and so he spent most of the day making his inquiries. It was five o'clock in the afternoon when he came back to his own boat again.

Stefek had wakened up an hour or two earlier and had spent the time since then trying to make himself look clean and tidy. He had washed the grey dust out of his hair and brushed the grey dust out of his clothes and scrubbed his face and his hands.

His leg felt much less painful but he was resting it when Jake arrived because he wanted to be able to walk again when night came.

"You look a sight better now," Jake said cheerfully as he came into the cabin. "That's good, that is. And I've got news for you."

He laid a bag on the table. "Present from a friend o' mine," he said. "Apple pie for our supper. Don't know when I last tasted apple pie."

He pulled the scarf tighter round his neck and sat down on the edge of the bunk.

"Now," he said, "that Wattie's a right rogue, it seems. For the past year or so 'e's been making a nuisance of 'imself in these parts. All kinds of thieving, that's 'is line. The bombs give 'im a great chance."

"Did you find out where he lives?" Stefek asked eagerly.

"Well, no," Jake admitted, "not just yet. But we will, don't you worry. My spies are out now and they'll report back. We'll find 'im!" He took out his pipe and began to fill it. "Don't you worry," he muttered. "Don't you worry."

Stefek had been hoping he would find Tadek that very night. But if it was not going to be possible, then he decided that he would go back to his plan of visiting Janey. For some reason which he did not clearly understand, he had begun to feel anxious about her. He had never liked leaving her with the Shark, though Aunt Sarah was kind enough. Now he wanted to be sure that she was all right. He made up his mind to go round to the Shark's house as soon as it grew dark.

He was afraid, of course, that the house might have been bombed. It was scarcely possible to turn a corner in London now without wondering if the buildings in the next street would still be standing. But there it was, looking safe and strong, with not even a window broken, as far as he could see.

He stood in the garden under Janey's window and it seemed to him as if a year or two had passed since he and Tadek ran away from his place. Yet how long was it really? Only a week and a day!

He started to climb the drainpipe, finding it much harder than usual because of his damaged leg. He was halfway up when the siren sounded. "Moaning Minnie again!" he thought, remembering what the woman had called it. He went on climbing.

At the top of the drainpipe he had to heave himself on to the roof and crawl up a short tiled slope to the flat bit under the window. This was easier to manage but, as he crouched there, he began to wonder whether the Shark was still refusing to let anyone in the house take shelter during a raid. Even the Shark couldn't be saying now that the Germans would never drop bombs on a place like Chelsea. So perhaps Aunt Sarah would be in there, behind the window, telling Janey to get up and go down to the cellar. Stefek hesitated. What should he do?

Moaning Minnie stopped, and in the silence that followed he put his ear to the window pane and listened. There was no sound from inside. So, after a moment, he tapped gently: one, two, three, and a pause, then one, two, three. Nothing happened.

She couldn't be asleep, could she? Surely the siren would have wakened her. All the same, he tapped louder. Still nothing happened.

Perhaps they were in the cellar already. But Moaning Minnie had started to howl only a few minutes before, so that didn't seem likely.

Stefek tapped again, more loudly than ever this time. When there was still no answer he tried to lift the window sash. It opened easily and he put his head through.

"Janey!" he called. "Janey, are you there?"

Nothing stirred in the room. But, as he listened, he heard sounds coming from the landing outside. At once he raced across to the door.

"Do be quick, Maurice!" said a woman's voice that he did not recognise. Certainly it was not Aunt Sarah.

"I'm coming, Hilda, I'm coming!" the Shark answered.

"Hilda?" Stefek thought. Who was Hilda?

"I do wonder where that child has gone," said the Shark, and his voice sounded nearer, almost outside the door. "It's very worrying to think of her out at night alone, and in an air raid too."

"She is a wild and foolish child," the woman replied, "and I agree that it's worrying but there's really not much more we can do about it, is there?"

Stefek heard their feet going down the stairs.

So Janey had gone. She had run away too, and he had missed her. Perhaps they would never find one another again. They were alone, all three of them.

Stefek blamed himself now for leaving Janey in this place. Where was Aunt Sarah? And who was Hilda, this woman with the hard and angry voice?

He climbed out on to the roof again, closed the window behind him and began to slither down over the sloping tiles.

Perhaps it was because he was upset and worried, perhaps because his right ankle was still not strong. Afterwards he did not really know what had happened. Somehow he lost hold and found himself sliding. He tried to grab at the gutter as he passed it, but he only succeeded in tearing his fingers on the edge. He landed with a heavy thud in a bed of earth and lay still.

For a moment he was stunned and dazed, aware of nothing but the shock to his huddled body. Then he began to wonder if he had hurt himself badly. What if he couldn't move? He cautiously tried his legs and they seemed all right.

119

Thankfully, he raised himself on one arm. That was all right too. He sat up.

The wind blew around him gently as he did so, and a bush rustled. He pushed his hair back from his eyes and moved the other arm. The elbow hurt, but ... What was that?

He had heard another noise, a crackle, like a twig breaking. Not the wind this time, that was sure.

He lay down again and held his breath. And a small figure passed by him, a few yards away, moving towards the foot of the drainpipe.

"Janey!" he whispered. "Janey!"

They could scarcely believe that they had found one another again.

"What are you doing out here?" Stefek whispered.

Then Janey explained why she had had to run away.

"But why did you come back?" Stefek asked her.

"I went so quickly," she said, "that I only had time to grab the puppy. I couldn't get up to my room for my gas mask, or my post office savings bank book or a coat or anything. So I thought I would wait till it was dark and then come back and climb up. See, here's the puppy! He's called Crackers but that's short for 'Fire-crackers' really. I found him in the middle of an air-raid, that's why."

The puppy licked Stefek's face.

"How were you going to climb up there holding him?" he asked.

"I wasn't," Janey explained. "I was going to tie him to the drainpipe. I asked a lady in a shop to give me a piece of string – and he's got his collar on. But now you can hold him."

Suddenly she looked at Stefek.

"Why are you sitting in the middle of the flower bed?" she said.

"I fell," he admitted. "I fell as I was coming down."

"Did you hurt yourself?"

"Not much. Not really."

"Hold the puppy, then," said Janey. "I won't be long."

She turned towards the drainpipe, then stopped.

"Which one are you?" she asked. "In the dark I can't tell."

"Stefek."

"Where's Tadek then?"

"I don't know," said Stefek. "Look Janey, get in there quickly and out again, then we'll go away from here."

"Where shall we go?" she asked.

"Don't worry about that," he said. "I've got a friend. We're going on board the *Daisy Belle*."

Chapter 25

The next morning they stood with Jake on the deck of the boat and watched the river as it slid past them towards the east, where the sun was climbing. The water glinted and gleamed. Along the river banks smoke from dying fires still hung like a peaceful early morning haze.

"Now, then," said Jake, "we're going to try again to find your brother."

"How?" Stefek asked.

"We'll go back to where you think Wattie lives, as near as you can remember, and we'll ask the people there about 'im. Somebody must know 'im. Now, you tell us where we start."

"Well," said Stefek, "I remember the name of the underground station where we took shelter. It was London Bridge. If we go back and start from there I might be able to follow the same road again, at least as far as the tobacconist's shop where we hid in the cellar."

"That's what we'll do, then," said Jake. "That's a good plan."

Jake thought they should leave Crackers on the boat, but Janey was worried in case he would become frightened if there was an air raid. So they took him with them. Janey carried him most of the time.

They went on an underground train to London Bridge and Stefek led them through the streets on the south side of the river, trying to remember every turn that he and Tadek had taken. But it was no use. After hours of searching they had not found the tobacconist's shop. All he could say was that they were in the right district.

"We need something to eat now," said Jake at last, and they went into a little café.

Jake ordered three cheese sandwiches, a biscuit for the puppy, a cup of tea for himself and lemonade for Stefek and Janey.

The waitress had a mass of fair hair that was frizzy from being too tightly curled. Behind small round spectacles her eyes were tired.

Jake said: "Cheer up, ducks! It won't last much longer, I reckon. Our boys'll 'ave 'em licked soon."

Stefek understood that "licked" must mean "beaten". He tried to remember the word for Tadek.

"I never believed it would ever come, you know," said the waitress, "not till it 'appened. Whoever *could* 'ave believed it would go on night after night, day after day, like this? Who would 'ave thought we could live with them bombs falling all round us and not go mad with fear?"

Jake nodded.

"The Jerries thought we'd go mad with fear," he said. "That's what they've been counting on."

The waitress stood up straighter and tossed back her head.

"The odd thing is, you find you can take it. Lord knows why, but you just carry on. And in a way, you know, things is better. People are kinder to one another in all this trouble. They helps each other more."

"I wonder," said Jake, "if you can help us?"

She looked surprised. "If I can," she said.

"We're trying to find a man called Wattie," Jake explained. "Lives around these parts, 'e does, but we don't know exactly where. Got a mop o' white curls, and sort of yellow teeth, and 'e ain't no Londoner. Scotch, 'e says. Big fellow. Ever seen 'im?"

As he spoke, the waitress turned away from them and began to wipe the cover on the next table. It was made of oilcloth, with a pattern of red and white flowers. She kept her eyes fixed on it.

"I might 'ave seen 'im around," she said cautiously.

"Don't you know where 'e lives, then?" Jake asked.

"No, 'fraid I don't," she said, still not looking at him.

"Do you think she knew?" Janey asked as they left the shop.

"She knew," said Jake. "More than she told us, anyway." He laughed. "Not even the bombs would make 'er 'elp people as much as that."

"Why wouldn't she tell?" Janey wondered.

"Maybe she's scared of 'im. From what you tell me, 'e could scare people all right, couldn't 'e? Well, this ain't gettin' us nowhere. We'll just ..."

He stopped suddenly in the middle of his sentence.

"Oh, well, 'ere we go again," he said as the air raid warning sounded.

They stood for a while looking upwards, watching.

At first the battle was high in the air, so high that they could hear very little sound. The bombers flew towards the north-east in straight lines. The fighters attacked them like little insects, in darts and loops and whirls. And the white trails

124

from the engines wrote the record of it all across the sky.

"Look!" Stefek yelled suddenly, pointing upwards and jumping with excitement. "We've got him! We've got him!"

They watched as one of the trails thickened and grew black, and turned downwards.

"You're right!" cried Jake.

The raider plunged towards the ground.

After that the planes all moved away, but then a new wave of bombers came in, much lower, and the anti-aircraft guns began to fire. Tiny puffs of smoke appeared in the air as the shells burst; and fragments of shell began to fall back on to the roofs and pavements.

Jake looked at the children.

"We'll 'ave to take shelter," he said. "Them bits o' fallin' metal are worse than the bombs."

They found a surface shelter, one of the kind built of brick with a flat concrete roof. Janey thought it did not look very safe, but they went inside and sat there quietly until the raid was over.

When they came out again, a warden stood by the door, a woman, small and thin. Her tin hat seemed much too big for her and she had tipped it back, letting a very strong face look out from beneath it.

They passed her and walked on, but Jake stopped suddenly.

"*She* might know 'im," he whispered. "The wardens get to know everybody on their patch. And *she* wouldn't be frightened of nobody, would she, now? Just look at 'er!"

He turned round and asked her.

"Yes," she said slowly, "I know the man you mean. I've had my eye on him for some time. Why do you want him?"

"Because 'e's got this kid's brother with 'im," Jake explained. "Can you tell us where to find 'im, please. It's urgent."

She frowned and looked at Stefek. He was at least as tall as she was.

"I could have told you until yesterday," she said. "But last night the building where he lived was destroyed. It was a direct hit."

Stefek felt his stomach grow tight with fear. He wondered if he was going to be sick.

Jake rubbed his chin and looked bewildered. Then he gave a little cough and he spoke again:

"Were there ... was anybody found?"

"No," said the warden, "I wasn't there when the rescue team went in, but I believe they found no bodies."

Chapter 26

"Now don't you worry," said Jake. "If there 'ad been any bodies, they'd 'ave found 'em. I expect Wattie and your brother were out during the raid. They'd be out searching for loot, I reckon."

"But even if that's true, where are they now?" Stefek cried. "And how are we going to find them?"

He was beginning to believe that he would never see Tadek again.

"Don't you worry," said Jake. He tightened his scarf around his neck and he spoke very firmly. "We'll find 'im. We're going off now to 'ead-quarters."

"What do you mean?" Stefek asked.

"We're going off to my mate's boat. Remember, I told you I 'ad my spies out? Well, that's the place they're reporting back to."

Jake took them to a boat that was moored at a jetty near Southwark Bridge. It was a much bigger boat than Jake's but it was not so clean and tidy. The paintwork was old and peeling, the brass had not been polished for many years. And now the soot and grime from the fires lay thick upon the deck.

"Ben!" Jake called. "You there, Ben?"

"Come aboard!" yelled a voice, booming up from below.

Ben was old, really old. He had a big bald head with a thin fringe of white hair round it, and he had a long white beard that straggled down over his seaman's jersey. He looked as though he had been very fat and had lost weight, for his clothes seemed to be too big for·him. He kept hitching up his trousers.

"There you are then, Jake, me boy!" he said. "I was wondering when you was goin' to show up again. Hullo! Who's this you've got with you?"

Jake introduced Stefek and Janey.

"So you're the boy that's lookin' for 'is brother, eh? Well, I've got news for you!"

Stefek's heart jumped. He was afraid to hope for too much.

"You see, son!" said Jake triumphantly. "I told you, didn't I? Come on then, Ben! Spill the beans!"

Stefek guessed at once what "spill the beans" must mean. "That's a good one," he thought.

Ben was speaking.

"Young Tommy Budge come back with the news," he said.

"Tommy Budge," said Jake. "Who's 'e?"

"Don't you know young Tommy Budge?" said Ben. "Not that 'e ever worked on the river

128

'imself, right enough. Seagoing lad, 'e is. But 'is dad was on the river, years ago. Sebastian Budge, you ain't forgotten 'im, 'ave you?"

Stefek could not stand it.

"Please, sir," he said, "what's the news?"

Ben looked at him as if he had quite lost hold of what they were talking about.

"The news? Oh, yes the news. Well, the fellow you're after — his place 'as just been bombed."

"We know that," said Jake quickly.

"You do?" Ben was disappointed. "Who told you?"

Stefek thought: "That's all he knows. It's hopeless."

"Air raid warden," Jake was explaining. "But she didn't know where 'e is now. So we ain't much further on, are we?"

"Aha!" said Ben. "You've forgot young Tommy Budge."

"Come on, then," said Jake. "Get on with it! Spill the beans!"

"That's what I've been trying to do, ain't I?" Ben muttered a little grumpily.

"Spill 'em," Jake commanded.

"Well," said Ben, "young Tommy Budge went asking questions in the *Green Dragon*. You know the *Green Dragon*, Jake?"

"Course I do," said Jake, who had been watching Stefek's face. "Get on with it Ben! The nipper can't stand it. What did Tommy Budge discover?"

Then Ben spilled the beans at last.

"There's a ship's come into dock," he said. "The cargo's just been unloaded into a warehouse. Wattie's tired of small jobs, 'e's impatient now. So 'e's coming tonight with a big truck to try to take this cargo."

"Now why would Wattie tell anyone if 'e was about to do that?" Jake asked a little cautiously.

"Because 'e's got to 'ave the truck and 'e's got to 'ave the juice, that's why. So 'e done a deal, and young Tommy got word of it."

"Do you know what ship and what warehouse?" Jake asked.

"Yes, mate, I do!" said Ben with great satisfaction.

Chapter 27

"Look at that!" Janey whispered. "What is it?"

A great bright orange-coloured light was falling slowly out of the sky across the river, making the moon seem pale.

"Don't you know?" Stefek answered. "It's a flare. The Germans drop them sometimes before they drop their bombs. It's supposed to let the airmen see what's underneath them."

"I don't know why they think they need them tonight, when the moon's nearly full," said Janey.

"I don't know either," Stefek replied. "There *are* quite a few clouds about, though. And I think I heard thunder."

They were crouching behind some barrels at the end of a long warehouse. Jake was with them. Tommy Budge was hidden at the back of a shed farther along the quay.

"Listen!" said Jake. And in spite of the noise of the planes and the anti-aircraft guns, they could hear a different sound, like the engine of a truck, close at hand.

"It might be an ambulance," Jake whispered, "but I don't think so. I think it's 'im."

The new noise was lost for a moment in the thunder of the bombs which followed the flare, and they all gazed anxiously across the water. When they looked back again, a truck was rolling along the dockside towards them. It stopped, went into reverse gear and backed up to the warehouse door. As soon as it was in position there the driver's door opened and a man jumped down.

"It *is* him!" Stefek whispered. "It's the Wolf all right."

"I don't see your brother, though," said Jake.

"No, but he might be round the other side."

"Wait a bit, then. We'll just watch for a while. See what happens."

The man moved out of sight beyond the truck. Then in a moment they heard a new sound, the sound of wood splintering.

"It's the door," Jake whispered. "I think 'e's got an axe."

"The door's made of metal," said Stefek.

"The *big* door's made of metal," said Janey, "but there's a sort of wooden hatchway farther along. I saw it as we came in."

The splintering noise stopped. For several minutes they could hear nothing and see nothing. Stefek wanted to creep forward but Jake stopped him.

"Wait a bit, just wait," he whispered.

Then they saw the Wolf again. He was standing near the tail of the truck smoking a cigarette. He was just standing there, doing nothing. And still there was no sign of Tadek.

Stefek began to think that the Wolf was alone. He found that his lips were dry with the strain of waiting and he ran his tongue over them to moisten them. As he did so, he heard a grating sound, like metal moving on metal, and the big warehouse door swung open.

At once the Wolf dropped his cigarette, ground it under his heel and moved into the building.

Jake shook his head.

"Still no sign of your brother," he muttered. "I

wonder where …"

And just at that moment Tadek appeared. He came out through the door, dragging something heavy. He was in the shadow of the truck and he was bent double, but instantly Stefek knew.

"There he is! There!" he whispered.

Behind Tadek the Wolf had come, carrying a box in his arms, moving quickly.

"Right then!" said Jake. "On you go!"

Stefek put his fingers in his mouth and gave a long, low whistle. Tadek stopped tugging for just a second, then went on as before.

"He heard!" Stefek whispered.

"Are you sure he'll know it's you?" said Jake.

"Certain! He'd know that whistle anywhere!"

But Wattie had heard the noise too. He dumped the box into the back of the truck and swung round suspiciously.

For a moment he stood there listening. Stefek could imagine the fierce eyes under the heavy brows, the big fists clenched. He hoped Tadek would get quickly out of range.

The Wolf glanced at Tadek and muttered something. Then he took a few cautious steps towards the end of the warehouse, looked back over his shoulder at the open door, and hesitated as if he was not sure what to do.

Jake said: "Now's the time!"

He pulled a whistle from his pocket and blew on it hard. And from farther off, along the quay, another whistle answered him.

"That's right, young Budge," Jake murmured approvingly.

The Wolf seemed to jump straight up in the air. Then he ran, shouting something as he went. He reached the cabin of the truck with a few great strides of his long legs. They waited for the sound of the engine. Instead they heard a roar of fury from the Wolf's lungs.

"What's up?" Jake whispered.

Then from somewhere in the darkness another whistle sounded and another. And suddenly there were footsteps thudding along the wharf, and voices. Wattie scrambled out of the cabin and ran.

"It's the *real* police!" said Janey. "And I think they've got Tadek."

"Then they can have me, too!" cried Stefek. He ran out from their hiding-place waving his arms.

Chapter 28

The room at the police station was cold and bare. They sat on a wooden bench against the wall and waited.

They had been given cocoa to drink about an hour before. The empty mugs, chipped and cracked, stood now on a tin tray on the table.

"It's ugly," Janey thought, looking at the worn brown linoleum, the green woodwork, the dirty yellow walls. "But I suppose the cells are even worse." She shivered.

"Well," said Jake, "I'm glad young Tommy Budge nipped off smartly. Sensible thing to do, wasn't it? Not much cop spendin' all the night in 'ere. Though come to think of it, it ain't no worse than a shelter, is it now?"

"Why don't they let us go?" said Janey. "Do you think they didn't believe us?"

"They must have believed that I stopped the Wolf from getting away," Tadek pointed out. "I showed them the ignition keys that I took while he had his back turned."

"So why are we here, then?" Janey asked again.

Tadek shrugged his shoulders.

Janey thought: "If they lock us up in the cells, they won't let us stay together. Perhaps they'll keep the twins together but not me. They'll put me in a separate cell, I know they will."

She remembered the Gestapo prison in France and she felt sick and scared.

Jake pulled his scarf a little tighter around his neck and began to sing:

"What's the use of worryin'?
    It never was worth while,
    So pack up your troubles in your old kit bag
    And ..."

The door opened and a police sergeant came in followed by a young constable. The sergeant was not the man who had questioned them earlier but an older man with a long thin face and grey hair. He sat down at the wooden table in the middle of the room.

The young constable quickly lifted the tray with the empty mugs and put it down on the floor in a corner. Then he stood near the door.

"Now," said the older man, "you have already told your story to P.C. Richards. I want to check up on a few details, that's all." He looked at Janey. "Will you please come over here, young lady?"

Janey came and stood facing him.

"What is your name?" he asked. And although he asked it in a pleasant way, it brought back to Janey strong and frightening memories of the Gestapo man who had questioned her in France. He had tried to seem pleasant too – to begin with. She gulped and found it hard to answer.

"Your name, please," said the sergeant again. He looked a little puzzled.

"Jane Elizabeth Longman."

"Thank you. Please sit down, Jane. When were you born?"

"April the 16th, 1930," said Janey and sat in the chair facing him.

"Do you have your identity card with you or your passport?"

She shook her head.

"What is your father's first name?"

Janey closed her eyes. With every word that this man spoke, she remembered the Gestapo man more clearly. The two of them did not look at all alike, it was the questions which made her think of that other time – questions about dates of birth and passports, questions about her father.

"His name is Peter," she said faintly.

"Right!" said the policeman. "Good! Now then, Jane, I want you to come with me!" And he stood up.

Janey thought, "They're taking me away to lock me up alone, I won't go!"

She got up and backed away from him, knocking her chair over. The young constable came forward and picked it up again.

"Dear me!" said the sergeant, looking more puzzled than ever. "Do I seem so frightening? There's nothing to be afraid of."

He muttered something to the constable, who nodded and went away. The sergeant sat down again.

Janey said: "We didn't help that man. We weren't stealing anything. We were only trying to rescue Tadek."

"Don't you worry, love," Jake whispered. "It's all right!"

"Jane," said the sergeant, "you haven't understood. It's just that there's someone who wants to see you."

"If it's my uncle, *I* don't want to see *him*," she replied.

"It's not your uncle," said the policeman, "it's ..." A knock on the door interrupted him. "Ah, here she is, I hope. Come in!"

The door opened and a young woman walked in, followed by the constable, who closed it and stood once more beside it. The woman was wearing a tightly belted raincoat with the collar turned up. She had brown curly hair, cut quite short, and her cheeks were pink, as if she was very healthy or as if she had just been running.

"Good evening," she said, her eyes moving around quickly from Janey and the policeman to Jake and the twins then back again. "No, it should be 'good morning' by now, shouldn't it?" She smiled and held out her hand to the police sergeant, who had risen to his feet. "I'm Nan Forbes."

"I'm very glad you've come," he told her. Then, looking down at Janey: "This is the young lady you want, Miss Forbes. There's no doubt about it."

"Good," said Miss Forbes, "I'm so pleased. I've been searching for you everywhere, Janey."

Janey stared at her. She had never seen this woman before, she was sure of it. The woman's face looked friendly but it was the face of a stranger. The stranger smiled but no one smiled back at her.

"Why?" said Janey sharply. "I don't understand. What do you want me for? Why have you been looking for me?"

"Because your father asked me to," the stranger told her.

Chapter 29

For a moment Janey was too surprised to speak. Her mind began to whirl with conjectures. Had this woman met her father in France, then? Or could it be that he was back in England? But if he was back, why hadn't he come himself to find her? Was he ill or something? Had he been wounded?

"Is he ... is he all right?" she cried.

Nan Forbes nodded and moved a step forward into the room.

"He's fine. There's nothing to worry about, Janey."

"Then what—?"

"I think we should all sit down," said Nan, "and I'll explain." She turned to the police sergeant. "May I have a few minutes here with them?"

"Of course," he said. "We'll leave you together." And he went away, taking the constable with him.

"That's better," Nan murmured as the door closed. She picked up the chair from behind the table, carried it round to the other side and sat down. Janey sat on the bench between Jake and the twins.

"Now," said Nan, "I'll explain. You see, your father and I both work for – that is, we both work in the same organisation. Do you understand?"

"I understand," said Janey. "You mean the Secret Service."

140

Nan laughed.

"Well, sort of, perhaps."

"Is he back in England?"

"No, he's not in England now, but sometimes he can send wireless messages. When he heard—"

"Could *I* send a message to *him*?" Janey asked quickly. Nan hesitated.

"Well, we'll see. Anyway, when he heard about all the bombing here, he began to worry about you. He asked me to try to get you out of town, safely into the country. But then your uncle told me you'd run away. So that was a bit of a problem."

She smiled and ran her fingers through her hair, thrusting it back behind her ears. Stefek decided that he liked her.

"Does my father know I ran away?" Janey asked.

"No, we didn't tell him. It seemed best to find you first. So we asked all the police stations to try to help, but we were very worried, we really were. Then only an hour ago—" She caught sight of Janey's face and stopped suddenly. "What's wrong, Janey? Don't you want to go into the country? I thought you'd like that."

"So I would," said Janey, "only ..." She glanced to her left where the twins were sitting. "It's just that ..."

"You don't want to leave your friends," said Nan. "But they're to go too, of course. Your father wanted all three of you to go." She turned to the twins. "You're Stefek and Tadek, aren't you? Would you like to go too?"

Before they could answer her, Jake spoke. He had been leaning forward with his palms on his knees, listening silently. Now he straightened up and rubbed his hands together.

141

"There!" he said in a contented voice. "That's it then, ain't it? That's settled!"

He sounded as if he was speaking the last lines in a play. But the twins were looking doubtfully at one another.

"Where would it be, please?" Tadek wanted to know.

"My brother has a house in the Scottish Highlands," Nan told him. "There's lots of room in it – and there are hills to run about on and boats to sail in. I think you'd like it."

Stefek and Tadek rose to their feet at exactly the same moment as if someone had given an order. They stood very straight, like soldiers. Stefek spoke.

"We came here to fight the Germans. We did not come to play about like children."

This sounded like lines from a play too, but quite a different play, one that was far from finished. Jake sighed.

Nan looked at the two figures, heels together, eyes to the front, arms stiffly by their sides.

"I see," she said. "Yes, I do see."

She had a leather shoulder bag, lying now in her lap, and she began to twist the strap between her fingers. Jake coughed and tightened his scarf. The boys relaxed a little but they went on standing side by side.

"Where do you want to go, then?" Nan asked.

"We thought ... back to Poland, maybe," said Tadek. But his voice showed that he was not sure.

"Would that be wise? Wouldn't you be better to stay free and fight later?"

"She's right, you know," Jake muttered.

"And Scotland's the place where most of the Polish soldiers are being sent for training," Nan added. "Did you know that? There are special

142

commando camps and that sort of thing. It might be a good place to be, later."

The twins glanced sideways at one another. Janey, watching closely, saw them make up their minds.

Stefek drew in his breath. "We'll go to Scotland, then," he announced slowly.

"That's it, then!" said Jake for the second time.

"I'm glad," said Nan, getting up from the chair. "And now do you know what time it is?" She looked at her watch. "A quarter past two! They wakened me at one o'clock to bring me here. Come along, then! We all need to get to bed."

"Thank you for asking us to go to Scotland," said Stefek as they left the room.

A police car drove them through the dark streets. The raid was over now and the city was quiet, but they could still catch the smells of gas and charred wood coming in to them occasionally through the open window and once they had to stop and take a different road when they came on a bomb crater in the middle of the street in front of them.

"Where are we going, please?" Janey asked.

"We're going to a flat owned by my family," Nan told her. "I don't live in it myself just now but there's someone there who will look after you till I can come and see you tomorrow. He's called Gordon. He was badly wounded at Dunkirk and he's a kind of caretaker now."

"Where do *you* live?" said Janey.

"In a mess," said Nan.

Tadek tried to choke back laughter then decided he hadn't heard properly.

"Excuse me," he said, "but *where* did you say you live?"

"In a mess," said Nan again. "Oh, I see! I'd forgotten you're Polish!"

Then they all began to laugh while Janey explained to the twins.

"It must be an *officers'* mess," she said. "You know, Tadek, that's the name for the place where army officers live."

"But are you in the army?" asked Stefek, when the laughter was over. "Even though you're not in uniform?"

"Yes," said Nan, "we're nearly all in the forces now."

Chapter 30

Janey slept until mid-day. What seemed to wake her was the sound of a clock chiming. Then almost at once there was a knock at the door and a man came in, limping badly as if one leg was shorter than the other.

"Better wake up now," he said, as he drew back the curtains. "Miss Forbes said to let you sleep as long as possible but the siren's just gone again. So you'd better get up and dress. Then we'll get you something to eat quickly and down to the shelter, I suppose."

"Are you Gordon?" said Janey.

"That's right, I'm Gordon. Now I think you ought to hurry. I've just been to wake the boys. They're getting up too. And, by the way, I think you'll like what you find in the kitchen when you get there."

What Janey found in the kitchen was Crackers. Jake had brought him along earlier that morning, having fetched him from Ben's boat where he had been left the night before.

"Where's Jake, then?" Janey asked.

"Oh," said Gordon, "he wouldn't stay. He just gave me the pup and went off. Said he had to get back to his own place."

Janey felt sorry she had missed him.

Gordon fried sausages for them all in the kitchen. As they ate, they looked out through the window at the sky and wondered what was going on up there, high above the clouds.

Nan Forbes did not come again till half-past eight that evening. When she arrived, the twins were in the kitchen with Gordon, who was telling them how he had been shot in the leg and the chest on the beach at Dunkirk, and how Nan's brother had picked him up and waded out with him to one of the waiting boats while the German planes roared and blazed around them.

"But he wouldn't come on board himself," Gordon said. "He just handed me over the side and went right back again to fetch some of the others."

"Your boat wasn't called the *Daisy Belle*, was it?" Stefek asked.

Gordon grinned. "It could've been called the *Queen Mary* for all I knew or cared as long as it floated."

Nan put her head round the door. This time she was wearing uniform.

"I'm sorry I couldn't get here sooner," she said. "Come on, you two. I want to talk to you."

Janey was in the hall trying to teach Crackers to sit when he was told. She was not having much success. She picked him up and followed the others into the room. Then she sat with him on the rug in front of the sofa.

"There's one thing I do want you to tell me," Nan was saying, "one important thing. Did you know what was in those boxes in the warehouse?"

It was Tadek who answered.

"Yes. There was wine in them."

Janey put the puppy down when she heard this and leaned forward.

"Right, so there was," said Nan. "But did you know before you went there, Tadek?"

"Yes, I knew. A ship from Portugal had

146

brought it in. That man Wattie told me in the end, though he wouldn't say at first."

The puppy went cautiously over towards Nan and sniffed at her ankle.

"Wattie said it was worth a fortune," Tadek added.

"So did you know who owned that wine? Any of you?"

The puppy took Nan's shoe lace in his mouth and began to chew it gently. Janey did not notice. She was watching Nan's face.

"No," said Tadek.

"No," said Stefek.

"It wasn't Uncle Maurice, was it?" said Janey.

Crackers pulled on the shoe lace hard so that the knot came undone. Nan bent down, tied it again, and picked the puppy up.

"Yes," she said, "that's right, Janey. You didn't know?" She looked from one to another. "No, you didn't, did you?"

"If I *had* known, I might not have wanted to save it from being stolen," Tadek muttered, half under his breath.

"You see," Nan explained, "the police were just a bit suspicious. You can understand that, can't you? They wondered if you were helping Wattie so as to get revenge on Mr Sharcus. But I'm glad you weren't."

"Why are you glad of that?" Stefek wanted to know.

"Because he's not a bad man really. He just cares too much about his wine, that's all. Oh, and I'm to tell you that your Aunt Sarah is back from hospital, Janey, and she'd like to see you. Will you go there tomorrow before you leave for Scotland?"

Janey nodded.

"We thought—" said Stefek, and stopped.

But Nan was looking at her watch and she didn't hear him.

"It's nearly time for the news," she said. "We shouldn't miss it tonight. Do you know that all day ..."

Stefek took a deep breath.

"We thought," he said, "that Mr Sharcus was a spy."

There was a moment of silence. Nan took her finger away from the puppy, who had been trying to chew it. Janey became aware of the clock ticking in the corner of the room. A bus passing in the street sounded its horn.

Then Nan gave a little laugh.

"You *what*? Mr Sharcus? Never!"

But she saw how the twins looked at one another. Putting the puppy down on the floor, she said: "All right, you'd better tell me."

"Well, he ... he goes out for a walk alone every night, even in the blackout," Stefek began. But even as he spoke, he found himself feeling slightly absurd. Going for a walk in the blackout did not seem now to be a very good reason for thinking a man was a spy. "We thought it was sort of ... sort of odd," he added uneasily.

"Yes," said Nan. "And what else?"

What else? The boys glanced at one another again. This time it was Tadek who tried to explain.

"You see, his name's funny. We thought that 'Sharcus' – well, it didn't sound *English*."

Nan smiled.

"How about *your* name?" she asked gently, and Tadek blushed.

Janey started to think then about her own suspicions of Uncle Maurice and all her fears

148

about his middle name, which she had not mentioned to anyone, not even to the twins.

"What really started all this?" Nan wanted to know.

"I think it was the poster about 'Walls have Ears'," Stefek explained, "and then a film that said there were spies everywhere and we were to look out for anything suspicious. So we tried to get evidence but we didn't manage it."

Suddenly Janey had to tell them. She spoke quickly and abruptly, blurting it out.

"I wondered about his name, too. His middle name begins with 'H' and for a while I got a funny feeling – I was just *sure* it was 'Hermann', you know like Hermann Goering. But in the end I looked in his passport and do you know what it is really? It's *Humphrey*!"

She stopped and laughed, her face very pink, and they all laughed with her. But still Tadek was not quite satisfied.

"I don't know," he said. "The passport could be a fake, couldn't it? Spies always have false documents. They have to."

Then Nan decided she had heard enough.

"It's time to stop this," she said firmly. "You mustn't go on imagining things. Now let's hear the news."

She looked at her watch again and switched on the wireless just in time to hear a voice saying:

"Here is the nine o'clock news and this is Alvar Lidell reading it. Up till eight o'clock tonight one hundred and sixty-five German aircraft had been destroyed in raids over this country."*

"Hooray!" yelled the twins.

"One hundred and sixty-five!" cried Janey.

Nan said nothing but her eyes were shining.

Then they listened and heard how wave after wave of German planes had tried to reach London that day; how Buckingham Palace had been hit though the bomb had not exploded; how a Dornier bomber had crashed to the ground just outside Victoria Station; and how people had been rushing to collect bits of parachutes to keep as souvenirs after German airmen were forced to jump from their machines.

When the news was over, Nan switched off the radio and turned to the children, her face serious and excited at the same time.

"It's an historic moment, I think," she said. "Do you know what that means?"

They shook their heads. Nobody was quite sure.

"It means that this is a time when things are happening that will change the whole of the future – things that people will remember forty years or fifty years or a hundred years from now. If Hitler had won the air battle that's been going on up there over our heads today, he might have

---

* The number of German planes shot down was really much smaller. The true figure turned out to be around sixty. Also the bombers came back later that night again. But it was still a great victory and a turning point in the war.

been able to invade us next week. But now I don't believe he'll dare to try."

"Will you be able to let my father know about this battle?" asked Janey.

"Oh, but he'll know," said Nan. "He was probably listening to that news bulletin just as we were."

Janey had not thought of this and the idea delighted her, for it seemed to bring her father near to her again. Nan came and sat on the rug beside her.

"He's all right, Janey. I can't let you know where he is but he's with friends."

Janey frowned slightly and picked at the pile of the rug with her fingers.

Tadek and Stefek had been listening silently. Now Tadek asked in a tentative voice:

"Will they be able to hear it in Poland as well?"

"Oh, yes," said Nan, "the news is broadcast to all the Allies, but the Germans try to stop people from listening, of course."

"People will listen in Poland just the same," said Stefek and Tadek, speaking exactly the same words together, as they sometimes did.

Nan nodded.

"I'm sure they will." She stood up. "But now it's time for bed, you know. You'll be travelling on the night train tomorrow."

"I want to look out first," said Janey.

"Why? Is there a special reason?"

"The sky up there, where they were all fighting. I just want to look at it. I don't know why."

They put the light out and crossed to the window. The sky over London was calm and clear and the full moon was shining.